Crooked Games

A Balum Series Western
No. 9

A novel by

Orrin Russell

Cover design and illustration by
Mike Pritchett

1

Balum sat upright before the morning dew had fully settled. The blankets he'd slept in fell away. The air was cold and still, silenced by low-hanging fog that stretched miles to the horizon, and he'd be damned if he was going to let that silence be broken by another morning of Joe and Valeria poking at each other in the tent beside him.

He pulled on his boots and slapped on his hat and slung his gunbelt around his hips. The ritual took three times longer than it should have; his left arm was wrapped in a home-made cast, and every time he twisted to the left, a stab of pain would shoot through his ribs.

He got up and walked past the ashes of the previous night's fire and gave the roan's nose a rub as he passed. He kept on, his footsteps silent. He crossed a hundred yards of dewy grass and stopped on a flat patch of sand and turned in a slow circle. He couldn't see more than thirty feet through the fog, but he'd lay a dollar there wasn't a living thing anywhere within it. Not a mole or a mouse, certainly not any game large enough to waste a bullet on. A scorpion, maybe.

They had only just cleared the deserts of Hell Country, and the grass they'd made camp in was the first they'd come to since riding out. It had been a week of eating dust, a week of ornery horses and scant food, a week of looking over their shoulders wondering if any of Big Tom's men were on their trail, if any of them were stupid enough or brave enough to put up a chase. It had been a week of pain; Balum's head still ached from the bullet that had carved a furrow along the edge of his skull. His ribs hurt, his arm hurt, and each night was an ordeal of twisting and turning on the cold desert sand, looking for comfort and not finding it.

It had been a week of awkward mornings too, that was certain. He felt like an intruder on a honeymoon.

He kicked the sand and spat. What he wouldn't give for a wad of chaw. A good fat wad of tobacco and a good spit. Two fingers of whiskey and a hand of poker, a plump woman to keep him warm, and a night without pain.

Things might have been more tolerable if Kiki or Chloe or even Josephine had stayed with them, but the dancehall girls had gone west to San Francisco, and Josephine back to Tin City. What Balum was left with was Joe, Valeria, and a string of thirsty horses. A fair degree of worry, also. Over one-thousand dollars in cash money was tucked away in his saddlebags; reward money for Buford Bell, which seemed an eternity ago.

The fog was starting to clear. He squinted through it and shook his head. If any of those fools from Big Tom's outfit were on their trail, he was in no shape to get into a shooting match. Not with his left arm in a cast, his head bandaged, and his ribs bruised yellow and black.

And not with the gun that sat in his holster either. It wasn't over.

"It's a new world we live in," said Joe. "The days of ball and powder are over. It's the age of the cylinder."

"I know it," muttered Balum.

"But?"

"But this just don't do it for me. It's too light, for one. It's got no heft. Feels wrong in the hand."

"You get used to things."

"Maybe." He looked toward the campsite. In the space between them the land rose and fell. He could see nothing of the tent and the horses and the fire. The coffee he could smell. He raised his chin at it. "She's a good woman."

"Don't I know it."

"You two need to get up the trail. Get on back to Cheyenne where you can be married."

"Balum, you know we're not getting married without you there."

"Still, you need to get moving."

Joe tilted his head. One eye narrowed. "What are you getting at?"

"I'm not getting at anything, I'm stating a fact. She's been through hell these last few weeks, and she doesn't need any more of it. I'm slowing you down. Next town we hit, I need to see a doc. Check out my arm, my ribs, my head. You two can go on without me."

Joe didn't answer. He stood there looking at Balum with his thumbs tucked in his gunbelt.

"Ah hell, Joe. I feel like a chaperone following a couple of lovebirds around. You two need some privacy."

Joe looked at his boots. A red blush came burning up his cheeks.

"Besides," said Balum, "ain't you worried about what might be coming up the trail behind us?"

Joe ran his black eyes over the horizon. "I was hoping that was my eyes playing tricks on me."

"Wasn't more than a puff of dust, but it was there."

"Could be the wind."

Balum raised his eyebrows. "You know it ain't the wind. You and me are both carrying a sight of money, and word gets around. Big Tom had several men who stayed back in Tin City. If they went looking for him, they'll have found out what happened. They'll have read the sign. They'll know I'm shot up, they'll know we have a woman with us, and they'll feel good about their numbers. So like I say, get Valeria up the trail where she's safe. Get back to Cheyenne. And tell Angelique I'm coming for her."

2

They entered the muddy streets of Inglewood six days later under black skies. Rain had begun to fall. The first few drops cut through the dust, which caked their clothes and browned their faces. It ran down their cheeks in thin crooked paths, and where it dropped from their boots, it dropped in thick rank globules into the rutted streets.

Alone in his room, Balum realized he'd been there before. It had only been two months ago; a one-night stay on his trip to San Antonio. The same hotel, the same room. The same bed. Only there was no Charlise or Cynthia to warm it. He listened to the rain patter the roof, and after a while he got up and went outside.

He found Joe sitting in a rocker on the veranda. It was an old rocker. It creaked as he pushed it.

"Doesn't look much different from when we first rode in, does it, Balum?"

It was true. It had been raining when they came through two months back with Buford Bell in shackles, and it seemed as if it had never quit. It fell in sheets, slapping the rooftops, throwing mud up against the storefronts. The town was infested with stray dogs, and their eyes glowed from where they cowered beneath the boardwalks.

Balum looked over the veranda and down the street where blackness sat like a thick dark curtain at the edge of town. "Whoever's out there is going to get good and wet."

"Soaked," said Joe.

"How many do you figure there are?"

The rocker squealed gently while Joe thought it over. "Three," he said. "Judging by the dust they were raising."

"That's about where I'd put it," said Balum. "I reckon they were two days behind us. This rain will make it three."

"Big Tom's men?"

"Yep." He turned his back to the street and leaned a hip against the railing. By habit he reached into his pocket for his tobacco, but his pocket was empty. "Damn." He looked around. "There's a saloon up the street. Let's go cut the dust out of our throats."

A smile touched Joe's eyes. He stopped the rocker. "Cut the dust?"

"Hell, just a quiet one, that's all. This town ain't big enough to get into trouble. Besides, Valeria could use a minute to herself. Ladies tend to appreciate that." He reached one foot out and tapped the rocker with his boot toe. "Come on," he said. "Let's go."

The town had but one saloon, and whatever its name was, the letters were long faded. The interior wasn't any larger than a two-stall cow barn and everything in it was as drab as the town in which it sat. Brown faded tables, a plank bar without a mirror. There was not a woman in sight, but the tables were filled with men, and more stood along the walls and lounged at the bar. When Balum and Joe shoved through the door with water pouring from their hat brims, every eye in the place swung onto them.

What they saw were two strangers, and two uncommon strangers at that. Balum stood several inches taller than the average man, wide in the shoulder and narrow in the hip, his face a testament to a life hard-lived; sun-burnt, wind-burnt, chapped by the heat and chapped by the cold, cut by fists, cut by knives. A rough-cut face that most men looked away from, and most women too. Out of nerves or fear or general politeness, he could only guess. But not all would look away. Some men would hold his eye. Young dumb pistoleros out hunting a reputation. Men who recognized him, or thought they did, men who'd heard stories of the *Cárcel de Belén*, stories of Lance Cain, Ted Turnbull, or any of the countless others. And there were women. Women who ran hot, who saw something wild and brutish in him and wanted it, wanted something untamed, something carnal and indecent. These women would hold his eye as well.

As for Joe, what they saw was a half-breed Apache standing nearly as tall as Balum, his hair long and black and his eyes blacker. He wore a Colt .45 at the hip and spurs on his boots. The sight of him would generally draw more eyes than were thrown Balum's way, and any cautious man would turn away as soon as he realized what he was looking at.

The men gathered in the Inglewood saloon that night were cautious men. They scooted their chairs aside to let them pass, and when Balum ordered two whiskeys, no one raised any objections to an Indian drinking in their midst.

They stood with their backs against the bar and they drank their liquor slowly, savoring it. Balum did what he always did; he looked each man over head to toe with special attention to their weaponry. He looked for other exits. He studied faces. He saw nothing worthy of note, and gradually he relaxed and let himself fade into the scenery, watching the poker games at the tables and idly considering taking a seat.

But he didn't. Not that he didn't have the money. Over a thousand dollars was tucked inside a satchel in his hotel room, and he had an even hundred on him right then. He was of no mind to lose it. He knew his skill as a gambler— Chester had let him know quite matter-of-factly. And so he watched instead.

When he finished his whiskey he ordered another.

Beside him Joe grinned. "I thought you said just one."

"You know it never works like that."

He'd just finished his third whiskey when the saloon door swung open and a short dirty man stumbled in dead drunk and nearly tripped into a table of card players. He straightened up and belched and excused himself, and wound a crooked path to the bar.

No one spoke to him. No one seemed to know him. He was mumbling to himself and through his mumbling he would sporadically hoot like a steam engine blowing his top. He squeezed in between Joe and Balum and slapped a palm over the bartop.

"Whiskey!" he bellowed.

The bartender scowled, but obliged him. The drunk raised the glass and held it to his nose and closed his eyes. He sniffed it. Whooped again. He tottered back a step and looked up suddenly as if he hadn't seen Balum standing beside him.

He squinted at Balum's empty glass. "Where's your drink, mister?"

"I'm all done for the night," said Balum.

"All done? There ain't no all done. Share a drink with me. You wouldn't have a man drink alone, would ye?"

He was standing too close and talking too loud, and his words were slurred and runny. Balum met Joe's eyes, and read them. Time to leave.

"Aw, wait now, wait." The drunk grabbed Balum by the sleeve. "I'm buying. Bartender! Pour this fellow here a whiskey!"

"I said I'm done."

"Nonsense! Celebrate with me. Look, I got plenty of money." He fumbled around beneath his overcoat and came up with his wallet. He pried it open and held it beneath Balum's chin. It was filled with cash. He could hardly close it. "I'll tell you what mister, I'm a lucky son-of-a-bitch tonight, and I'll tell ye why." He shoved a finger in Balum's chest. "Outside town there's an outfit driving cattle north. Bunch of cowpokes. Well sir, I set down with 'em and played one hand after another, and as God is my witness, I couldn't lose. No sir! Couldn't lose. Look here." He fumbled around again inside his overcoat and brought out a deck of cards. "I won every last penny off 'em. I even won their deck of cards!" He bent his head back and let out a roar.

"Let's go, Balum," Joe said.

"Hey, wait a minute," the drunk stepped in front of them.

"Do you think you're too good to let me buy ye a drink? You think you're better than me?" He waved the deck of cards extravagantly through the air. "I'll tell ye what. Let's play for a drink. Best hand wins. I'm warning you though, I can't lose today." He began a messy shuffle and immediately dropped several cards. He bent and scooped them up and stepped to the bartop and dealt out five.

"Come on, Balum."

Before Balum could take a step, the drunk grabbed up one of the two dealt hands and shoved them into Balum's chest. The movement was awkward, and in the process he revealed the hand. Four kings.

"Take 'em!" shouted the drunk. "Or are you yellow?"

Balum took them. Four pretty kings sitting all in a row.

The bartender set the two whiskeys over the bartop, and the drunk fumbled around again for his wallet. In the process he turned his own cards over. It was only a brief mistake, but it was enough. The hand consisted of three jacks and a couple of odd cards.

"Now see here, you high-falootin', too-good-to-drink, scoundrel," sputtered the drunk. "Why don't we make it interesting?" He pulled a wad of cash from his wallet and counted out ten dollars. He slapped them on the bartop. The saloon had gone silent. Every eye in the place was on them. "Well, sonny? Have ye got the balls, or don't ye?"

Joe was shaking his head. Balum ignored him. He reached in his pocket and slid out ten dollars. "Fine. There it is. Count it if you'd like."

The drunk grinned. An odd glint came into his eyes. He

didn't even look at the money. "Alright," he said. "How many cards, sonny?"

Balum looked at the deck. The drunk hadn't mentioned it would be draw poker. But it didn't matter. Balum couldn't lose. The drunk could exchange his two odd cards, and even if he came up with another jack it wouldn't beat Balum's four kings.

"I'll stay," said Balum.

"He'll stay!" the drunk mimed. His eyes widened and he looked around the saloon at the men gathered there. He mumbled something under his breath and he looked at his cards again. "I'll draw two for my own self."

He placed two cards face-down on the bartop and pulled two fresh ones off the top of the deck. No sooner had he seen them than he let out a whoop and a drunken belch. "Ohhh, boy," he shook his head. "You're time is up, sonny." He reached a finger out and poked Balum in the chest again. "I told ye I can't lose tonight. I'm gonna stomp ye like the high-falootin' son-of-a-bitch I see ye for. Want to see these cards?" He wiggled them over his chest. "It'll cost ye."

He pulled out his wallet yet again and grabbed a wad of cash. The bills fell over the bartop, and each one that fell would be accompanied with a slurred count.

"Forty!" he shouted when he reached it. He tucked his wallet back in his overcoat and wrinkled his nose at Balum. "Well? Or did your mammy dress ye in ladies' knickers this morning?"

The drunk had drawn his fourth jack and Balum knew it. He pressed his thumb into his four kings. Fifty dollars was nearly two months' of cowhand wages, and there wasn't a man in that bar who didn't know it. Hell, Balum knew it. He'd worked the line for less. To take a man's money like that, drunk as he was, it wasn't right. If it was another man or another situation… but it wasn't. This fellow was a damn fool, and he could use a lesson.

Balum snaked out his own billfold and peeled off forty dollars. It was an awkward process with his left arm wrapped up in the cast, but he managed. He laid the forty dollars across the plankboard bar and looked the drunk in the eyes, then he flashed a smile at Joe and spread his cards face-up beside the bills. The crush of men around him let out a collective murmur. Oohs and ahhs. Eyebrows raised. Balum shrugged and wrapped his arm around the two piles of cash, but the drunk caught him by the wrist and stopped him with a tsk and a shake of his head.

The crowd hushed again. The drunk laid his cards upon the bar and flipped them face-up, and in the space of the drop of a coin, the rabble broke into a clamor of shouts and whistles and wild drunken profanity. The man had not exchanged his two odd cards in hopes of drawing the last jack. Instead he had given up two jacks. What lay on the bar were the nine through king. All clubs. All in a row.

"Straight flush beats four-of-a-kind, sonny. Beats it every time."

The drunk swept the cash into a pile, straightened it, plucked up his deck of cards, and shoved it all into his overcoat. Then he tipped his hat and stepped through the crowd and sauntered out the saloon door and into the driving rain.

3

Balum set a hand over his chest where the drunk had poked him. His ribs were still bruised. They were giving him more trouble than his arm was, and the drunk's poking hadn't helped any. He swore under his breath. Beside him, Joe was eyeing the door.

"Something wasn't right about that, Joe."

"I could name half a dozen things."

"He looked drunk as a loon when he came in, but he walked out sober enough. I just don't see how—"

"Gentlemen," the voice was deep and fluid and interrupted Balum like a cat's purr. "Allow me to buy you both a drink. I saw the whole thing from start to finish, and if I say so myself, you could use it."

Balum turned. A tall man. Dark hair, clean smile. A carefully manicured mustache rode his upper lip. He wore a gabardine suit with silver buttons, his hat was of an eastern cut, and before Balum had fully taken him in, he'd called across the bartop for three whiskeys.

While the bartender poured, the man made introductions. Samuel Kingston. Land surveyor. He was making his way west on behalf of American Railcars Limited, and the town of

Inglewood was just one more stop along the way.

"Some days a man's luck has no ceiling," he was saying, "and today is such a day for that fellow."

"Maybe," said Balum. "But I get the feeling I've been swindled."

"Oh no," said Kingston. "It's luck, alright. I saw it myself just outside town where a crew of Texans have a herd of cattle bedded down. I rode up and stopped to ask directions, and that fellow was sitting with them by the fire, drinking and gambling and carrying on. I couldn't help but watch. I'll be damned if he didn't win nearly every hand he played. He won their last dime off them, and when their money was gone they bet the deck of cards, and he won that too." He shook his head. "Wildest bit of gambling I've seen in my life. Until this here, maybe."

Balum only grunted. His damn ribs were burning, and the whiskey wasn't helping. Then again, it wasn't making things any worse. He took another swallow.

"When one man's luck turns north, another man's turns south," Kingston said. "It's the way of the world. Lord knows my luck has gone sour."

Balum eyed him. "Is that right?"

"This is one of the most unfortunate nights of my life," said Kingston. He lowered his eyes into his whiskey, and said no more.

Balum looked at Joe. The Apache's black eyes held no sign one way or another.

"What happened?" said Balum.

Kingston looked up from his drink. "You might only laugh

if I told you. It doesn't seem such a serious thing."

"Try me."

"Well," Kingston took in a long breath of air and slowly exhaled. "It's about a watch. A pocket watch I keep right here close to my heart." He patted his gabardine suit with his free hand. He looked Joe in the eye, then Balum. "It just so happens I've lost it."

"You lost a watch?" said Balum.

"Indeed."

"And that's the most unfortunate night of your life?"

"I warned you that you might only laugh. But allow me. The watch in and of itself is of high quality; gold-plated and made with expert craftsmanship. It's easily worth twenty dollars. But to me it's worth much more. You see, fitted into the lid is a portrait of my dear mother. A daguerreotype. It's somewhat faded, but it's the only thing I have to remember her by. The only thing at all, and now it's gone. I've looked everywhere." His eyes dropped into his drink again. "Everywhere."

"Did you check that cattle outfit outside town? Maybe you dropped it."

"It's not there. I had it here, right inside this saloon not but an hour ago. I know it; I checked the time when I arrived. Somehow I've misplaced it. What I wouldn't give to have it back."

"Well," said Balum. "If I see it I'll let you know."

"Would you?" Kingston's eyes brightened. "If you were to find it and return it, I would gladly pay you. As I said, it's worth much more to me than a simple watch. Why, I would give you one-hundred dollars in reward. One-hundred, and it would be worth every penny to me."

"That's mighty generous."

"I'm staying at the hotel here in town. Room number one." He set his empty glass back on the bar and tipped his hat. "Now if you gentlemen will excuse me."

Balum watched the man turn and strut back through the crowd to the door. It was still raining outside, and he saw Kingston put a hand to his hat just as the door closed behind him.

Joe raised his eyebrows.

"What?" said Balum.

"You sure you want to stay on here? This town is full of kooks."

"I need to see a doc. Something's wrong with my ribs. And I need to get this cast off, too."

Joe shrugged. "You ready?"

"I'm ready."

They set down their glasses and began to push their way through the crowd when the door swung open and the same drunk as before stumbled in, short and wild and making a scene. He was grinning and hooting and elbowing forward toward the bar, and when he saw Balum and Joe he stopped and grinned at them with his head cocked sideways.

"The big loser!" he said, and he threw his head back and laughed. "Oh, don't look so sour. You're an unlucky man tonight, that's all. Happens to everyone. I'll tell you what. I'll make it up to ye. Let me buy ye a drink."

"No thank you," said Balum.

"Don't be sore. Come now, it's on me; I'm the lucky one. Hell, my luck just don't run out. Not tonight it don't. First the cowpokes, then you, and then, wouldn't you believe it, I go and find some dandy's watch laying in the mud!" He reached into his overcoat and pulled out a gold watch on a chain. "Just look at it! Why, it must be worth twenty dollars. By God, I'm going to buy the whole saloon a drink! Come on," he waved toward the bar. "Come with me. I'm buying."

"Hold on," said Balum. "Let me see that watch."

"Oh no you don't. Finders, keepers."

"Show me what's on the inside."

"What's on the inside? Why it's two little hands and a bunch of numbers, that's what's on the inside."

"Open it up," said Balum. "I'd just like to see."

The drunk weaved unsteadily a moment, then wiggled his head and flipped open the watch cover. Inside was the daguerreotype. Faded, but visible.

"I'll tell you what," said Balum. He kept his voice low, steady. He could make his money back if he was smart about it. Hell, he could make more than his money back. "You reckon that watch is worth twenty dollars, do you?"

"Damn right I do."

"Well like you say, your luck just won't quit today. I'm a man that prizes a good watch, and I'll give you twenty right now for it. Cash."

The drunk stepped back. He looked at the watch and he looked back at Balum and measured him from head to toe. "You don't look like no watch-wearing kind of man."

"Well I am."

The drunk pursed his lips together. He narrowed his eyes. His nose was dripping, and he wiped a sleeve across it. "No," he said finally. "I think I'll keep it for myself."

"Wait," Balum stepped closer. "I'll give you thirty."

"Thirty dollars?"

"Right now."

Again he narrowed his eyes. Studied the watch. The image. "How's about forty?"

Balum dropped his hand into his pocket. Just over forty dollars was all that remained. "Alright," he said. "Forty."

The drunk laughed. "I thought you were just an unlucky sort. Now I'm starting to figure ye for a fool. What's so special about this here watch?"

"I just want it," said Balum. "Hell, maybe I'm just drunk. Give me a few whiskeys and I don't make the best decisions. Forget it," he turned back to the door.

"Ho now," blurted the drunk behind him. "Hold up. If it's forty you'll pay, I won't stop ye." He held the watch by the chain and let it dangle. "By God, I'm a lucky man tonight."

4

The rain had dwindled to a sprinkle but the wind blew harsh across the muddy streets, and Balum bent into it with one hand tight to his hat and the pocket watch snug in his pocket.

They entered the small hotel reception and flicked the water from their hats, then entered the narrow hallway boasting rooms on either side. At room number one Balum stopped and raised his knuckles before the door, but Joe stopped him.

"Shouldn't you wait until morning? It's late."

"I'd rather do this now."

Joe shrugged. "See you in the morning, Balum."

When the Apache had disappeared into his room, Balum rapped his knuckles on the door. He waited. He lowered his hand into his pocket and rested it over the watch. He couldn't believe his luck. He didn't feel bad, not in the least. The drunk had done something shifty with that deck of cards, there was no doubt about that. This watch situation simply rectified matters.

He raised his hand again and knocked, this time louder. Nothing stirred. No light showed under the door.

"Come on," he muttered. He knocked again.

A light flickered on. Candlelight, soft and flickering at the toes of his boots.

The door swung open. A woman stood in the frame. She held a candle on a plate in one hand, and with the other she pinched the lapels of her satin nightgown tight across her breasts.

Balum stepped back. He swallowed. At over six feet tall, he weighed a good hundred and ninety pounds, and this woman, standing half a foot shorter, probably outweighed him by ten. She carried a good deal in her breasts and hips, but plenty everywhere else too; her thighs and belly, a little roll of fat in her neck. Her hair was tousled and her eyes half-asleep. She looked quizzically at him with her lips half-parted.

"Yes?" she said.

"Evening, ma'am." He removed his hat. "Is the mister in?"

"The mister?"

"Kingston. Samuel Kingston."

She blinked a couple times, waking up. "I'm afraid you have the wrong room."

"The wrong room?" He looked at the door. The number was drawn on the frame in black ink. "Isn't this room number one?"

"Yes, but there's no Mister Kingston here. No Mister Anybody. Only me." She shifted her weight from one foot to the other. Her hip jutted out, and a white swath of flesh showed beneath the nightgown.

"Well I…" He looked at the painted number on the door again and back at the woman, whose nightgown seemed even looser now, exposing more flesh, mounds of cleavage, the white of her thigh bare in the candlelight. "I'm sorry, ma'am." He tipped his hat again. "I beg your pardon."

Before she closed the door she let her eyes drop down over his shoulders and down his waist to his pants, his casted arm, his gun, clear down to his boots. Then she closed it.

In his room again, Balum sat on his bed and took out the watch and flipped it open. The rain had stopped. Through the clouds the moon shone, and by its light he studied the daguerreotype. Then he closed it. Dumb watch. It probably wasn't worth more than a dollar.

It came to him slowly then, in pieces. The puzzle. Putting it together. He didn't know how exactly the short man in the overcoat had gotten himself a straight flush, but it wasn't luck. And he hadn't been drunk. He realized then that the four kings had been planted from the start. How the drunk had "accidentally" shown both hands before the bet was made. And then the watch nonsense. How conveniently it had all played out.

Goddamnit, he was a sucker. A mark. He was out a hundred dollars, and somewhere close by were the men who'd fleeced him, laughing, sharing a drink together, counting their money.

He considered going after them, but he'd never find them. Not in the dark, not in the rain.

He kicked off his boots and unbuckled his gunbelt. He sat back down. He couldn't stop going over the pieces. Was the barman in on it? The cowpokes? The gamblers? The general rabble that had stood by and watched it happen?

He undressed and laid down on the bed and closed his eyes, but he couldn't sleep. His ribs hurt. He sat up suddenly.

The woman. Room number one.

It made no sense that she would be staying in this run-down hotel in this mutt-infested town, not a woman like that, not alone. And what kind of a woman answers a knock on the door in the middle of the night half-naked? She was fatter than a suckling pig, but goddamn if she hadn't distracted him. All that flesh. And that was the point; to distract him.

He stood up. He felt around for his trousers, pulled them on with one arm, then searched the dark for his boots and tripped over them. While he shoved his feet inside he considered that he'd just drunk four whiskeys and that every one of them had been a heavy pour. Just more reason to think the barman had been a part of it. But no matter. His judgement wasn't clouded. Hell, it was obvious, all of it, the whole damn thing.

He got his casted arm through his sleeve and buttoned his shirtfront, then slung his gunbelt around his hips and stepped into the hallway. On the floor his footsteps made no sound.

At room number one he stopped and slid the Colt from its holster. He turned the butt to the door and raised it, then paused. Why knock? Surprise was what he needed.

He lowered it. Put his hand on the knob.

It turned easy in his hand, unlocked, and he threw it open and stepped into the room and slammed the door closed with his foot.

By the moonlight streaming through the window he saw the woman on the bed. At the slam of the door she jerked awake. She let out one high-pitched squeal and sat up and yanked the blanket over her chest.

"Alright," Balum swung the barrel of the Colt from one side of the room to the other. "Where is he?"

"What?" She pulled the blanket tighter.

"Where's Kingston? Where's the short man in the overcoat?"

"What are you talking about?"

Aside from the bed, the room contained an armoire and a small desk. The furniture cast shadows in all directions. Balum swung the gun from one shadow to another, half-expecting a figure to rise up from one of them. The candle sat on the desk, matches beside it.

"Light that candle," he said.

She didn't move.

"Light it."

She let the blanket go. She stood up. Her nightgown hardly covered her. When she came around the edge of the bed he caught the shape of her rear end in the moonlight, the crease where her butt met her thighs. For as much flesh as there was, it was tight and smooth and perfectly shaped. She lit the candle and turned to face him.

"You're going to tell me where those men are, or I'll walk you across the street and toss you in jail, and you can stay there until I find them. So talk."

She looked him over in the candlelight. The same look she'd given him before; head to toe. "What in the world are you going on about?"

"You know what. Those men. Tell me where they are."

"I have no idea what you're talking about."

"Yes you do." He took a step closer.

"I don't. And I can't honestly believe you're going to take me to jail, either."

She walked forward as she said it, stating it like a challenge. She came right to the edge of the bed, not two feet from Balum. She put her hands on her hips, which allowed her satin nightie to inch further down her bosom.

"Nothing," she said. "That's what I thought." She turned slowly back around and lifted a knee onto the bed. "I'm going back to bed."

She crawled slowly onto the edge of the bed and paused there kneeling on the mattress, then turned her head and looked over her shoulder. The lace hem of her nightie had shimmied up her waist, and half of her ass was bare and sashaying in front of him; one cheek white in the moonlight, the other orange from the glow of the candle.

He reacted without thinking.

He grabbed her around the waist with his casted arm, and when the palm of his free hand smacked her ass, the sound was sharp like the crack of a whip. She let out a squeal and her body jerked, and immediately Balum spanked her again.

"Where are they, huh?" He shook her with his casted arm. "Where'd they go?"

She sank to her forearms. His arm was wrapped beneath her belly, and when she sank down she nearly pinned him there. He gave her another spanking, which elicited another squeal. He tried again. Then again. Her ass rippled each time his palm landed. The hem of the nightie had fluttered up around her waist, and all she wore beneath it were a pair of red panties as delicate as any he'd ever seen.

He landed his palm again, but her response was more an 'oooh' than anything else. Her head was turned sideways on the mattress and she was looking back at him and breathing heavy, her mouth wide open and her eyes locked on his.

He raised the flat of his hand again, and paused. She wasn't struggling. She wasn't trying to get away, she wasn't screaming for help. She gave her ass a little wiggle.

He pulled his arm out from under her belly and stepped back.

The smell of sex was everywhere, the smell of pussy. She was still looking at him, her ass arched in the air, bare but for the red thread of panties lost in the folds of her flesh.

"Ack," he growled, and turned away.

He went to the door and jerked it open. In the hallway he turned to close the door and he caught one last sight of her kneeling on the bed on all fours, her ass in the moonlight, mouth open, panting. Her hair hung around her face in loose curls, and through it her eyes met his. She let one last little whimper escape, then he slammed the door shut behind him.

5

The whistle of the train woke him. He jerked upright and immediately brought his fingers to his temples. The effects of the whiskey sat there like a vice across his eyes. He rubbed them and swung his feet off the bed. His boot heels landed hard on the floor; he'd slept in his clothes.

He stood up and went to the window just in time to see the train pull away. The steam whistle screamed again and a puff of black smoke billowed out the chimney.

He was hungover and he'd overslept, his ribs hurt like the devil, and he felt about as ornery as a man could feel when he walked out of the hotel and onto the miserable drag of Inglewood where stray dogs ran like packs of wolves through the mud. They were running through the alleyways and snarling at each other in the middle of the street, and when one bared its teeth at Balum, he shooed it off with the toe of his boot.

"Don't get bit, now, Balum."

He looked up. Joe was adjusting his saddlebags. Valeria was already mounted in her saddle, ready to go.

"Morning," said Balum. "Say, you reckon there was something wrong with that whiskey last night? It feels like someone hammered a nail through my skull."

Joe grinned. "That's what rotgut whiskey will do to a man."

"You don't figure that barman put something in it?"

"Like what?"

"Hell, I don't know. My mind's been running. Seems like the whole town was in on it."

Joe shook his head. "They weren't. Tell him, Valeria."

She looked radiant, sitting tall in her saddle with her hair as black as Joe's. A senorita, beautiful and misplaced in that miserable town. She smiled at Balum. A warm smile, a touch of humor in it.

"I know them," she said. "They operate a traveling carnival. There are several more that work with them, but the people in this town are not part of it. Kingston runs it all. The short man is Barney Harrington. They came through Tin City a couple of times, and after they'd conned a few people out of their money, Big Tom ran them out."

"Who's the woman?"

"What woman?"

"The one working with them. She's a big curvy girl, pretty, maybe twenty-five years old."

Valeria's eyes drifted down, trying to remember. "I never saw a woman with them. It's just men, as far as I know. They're good at what they do— they're professionals. They know more ways to fleece a man than any of the parlour girls at Big Tom's place ever did. It's when they set up their carnival show that they really clean up. There isn't an honest game in the whole thing."

"No woman?"

"Not that I ever saw. There's a cardsharp named Rhett Hastings that's mixed up with them. Whatever you do, don't play poker with him if you run into him."

The mutt at Balum's feet was still snarling. He jabbed at it with his foot and finally stepped away. "Well they had a woman with them this time. Whoever she was, she's gone on the train, I can guess that much. Them too, most likely."

Joe finished adjusting the saddlebag and swung up. "You sure you want us to go on without you?"

"I'm sure. I need to see that doc. Besides, you two need to put some distance between yourselves and whoever's coming up the trail."

Joe narrowed an eye at him. "Will you manage to stay out of trouble?"

Balum snorted. He rubbed a hand across his stubbled jaw and flashed a finger out suddenly. "Wait a minute," he said, and stepped back into the hotel.

When he came out he was holding the satchel where over one-thousand dollars in bounty money was encased. He held it out.

"Take it," he said. "The fact is, I can't stay out of trouble. You know that as well as I do. I want you to take it up to Cheyenne and give it to Angelique. I trust her more than I trust myself."

"Are you sure?"

"I'm sure. I took some out for myself. Enough to make the trip, but no more. You two go on now. You've got a lot of ground to cover."

No one moved for a minute. They shared a look, a long one that held in it years of friendship, memories of campfires and cattle drives, nights of whiskey, and more than a few battles. Gunfights and knife fights, death and violence.

Joe put a hand to the brim of his hat and tipped it. "We'll see you in Cheyenne, Balum."

"See you there," he said, and gave Joe's horse a swat on the rump.

The horses took off in a trot down the muddy lane, dogs snipping at their heels. They reached the end of the drag and turned north into the grass, and disappeared beyond the last few buildings there.

Balum set his fingers against his ribs. He needed that doctor bad, but there was an order to things, and he knew what it was.

The sign over the jail had not been fixed. It hung by two nails, and whenever the wind blew it would smack against the facade. He crossed the street and pulled the door open and found Old Man Pickens sitting at the desk with his feet propped over the top. He jerked them down and onto the floor at Balum's sudden entrance.

"You in a hurry to fix that sign out front, or do you have a minute?"

The sheriff tilted his head and scowled. "You again," he said.

"You remember."

"How the hell would I forget?" The sheriff glanced out the small warped windowpane and back at Balum. "You bringing trouble again? Last time you came through I got hogtied and tossed around like a bum. I don't fancy another round of that."

"It worked out alright though, didn't it, Sheriff?"

"I don't know. Did it? What happened to that fellow you were escorting? Buford Bell, was it? What became of him and his lousy brothers?"

Balum pulled out the free chair beside the sheriff's desk and sat down. The old sheriff had a right to be riled up. Two months back, Buford's' brothers had clocked him over the head, bound him in rope, and dragged him several miles outside of town. He must have looked like a fool to the townsfolk. Then again, he didn't size up much as a sheriff, either. He'd seemed nothing more than an angry old man when Balum first met him, and he didn't seem much different now.

"Dead," said Balum. "All of them."

The sheriff huffed through his nose. "Good riddance," he said. "A few less bums in the world."

"There's plenty more bums to take their place. That's why I've come to see you. There's a few men riding up the trail, and they're bringing nothing but trouble with them."

"Who?"

"Hired guns. They worked for a man named Big Tom, and now that he's dead I expect they want revenge or money, or who knows what. They're about a day down the road. I expect they'll ride in tomorrow."

Sheriff Pickens let his shoulders slump. "Can't you deal with them yourself? Weren't you appointed U.S. Deputy Marshal?"

"On a temporary basis. That's over now."

"Well what do you want me to do?"

"I'm in no shape for a fight, you can see that," Balum raised his broken arm. "Best thing would be to catch them as soon as they come in and throw them straight into a cell."

"Based on what?"

"I don't give a damn what you base it on. On anything. Just put them away for a while until I'm clear of here."

"And when will that be?"

"That depends."

"Depends on what?"

"On how quick your doctor is."

Sheriff Pickens' eyes shot to the cast.

"If he's quick," said Balum, "and he patches me up, I'll be gone soon enough. In the meantime, if you're looking for something to do, you can go hunt down the folks conning people out of their money."

"What folks?"

"Couple fellows and a woman. They were here last night, working folks over. They worked me over. I guess there's a cattle outfit outside town, seems they fleeced them pretty good too."

"There's no cattle outfit outside town."

"No?"

Sheriff Pickens shook his head. "I'd know it if there was. Fact is, the grass around here is no good. Nearest cattle trail is a good hundred miles east of here. The only thing outside town is that traveling carnival show. They don't set up for towns this small though."

Balum put his fingers to his temples again. The whole damn thing had been a lie. Valeria was right— they were good at what they did; he'd give them that much.

"Well," said Balum, "they're gone now. I'm sure of it. I'll come looking for you tomorrow morning, early. We'll catch Big Tom's boys before they reach town."

The sheriff began to sputter a series of protests, but Balum had already turned to the door. Before he reached it he caught a look out the window. He flinched suddenly, and wheeled back a step.

She had just come out of the hotel and was taking dainty steps through the mud toward the ramshackle cafe down the lane. The dress she wore was of an eastern cut, the envy of many a homely woman in the west, and whether it was cut unreasonably low in the bust or her chest was simply too ample to fit inside, either way she was spilling out.

Balum stuck his nose to the window and watched her take a few more steps, then swung around to Sheriff Pickens.

"That's her." He jabbed a finger at the window.

"Who?" Pickens craned his neck up.

"Right there, going into the cafe. She was part of it, I guarantee it."

The sheriff scrunched up one side of his face and cocked his head sideways. He looked at Balum the way one would regard a madman raving in the streets. "Part of a con job?" he laughed. "That, Balum, is Ms. Lexi DeVries. She came down from Cumberland a week ago on her way to San Antonio, and not but a mile outside town her wagon broke. The rear bolster come loose, or some such thing. It's sitting there now, waiting for Eli to get back from wherever he done run off to, to fix the dang thing." The scrunch hadn't left his face. He eyed Balum a minute, then added: "Eli Brown, the only carpenter from here to Cumberland."

Balum threw another look out the window, but the woman was gone. "Are you sure about that?"

"Am I sure about that? Shoot." He threw his feet back over the desk and laced his fingers together behind his head. "You ain't stirring up no trouble with that good woman, are you?"

In his mind he could hear the slap of his palm on her ass. Her squeals. The smell of her panties.

"I ain't stirring up no trouble."

6

The doctor's office was situated opposite the cafe, and when the doctor opened, he opened with a flask of whiskey in hand. He adjusted his spectacles and gave Balum a quick look up and down. Then he waved him inside.

"Sit there," he motioned to a squat table covered in red-checkered cloth.

Balum sat. He watched the old doctor shuffle over to a sidetable and carefully put his flask down, then shuffle back, inching his spectacles back up the bridge of his nose.

"What can I do for you?"

"I'd like to see about getting this cast off," Balum raised his arm. He took off his hat and pointed out the furrow where Big Tom's bullet had caught him. "There's this, too."

"Mm hm," grunted the doctor.

"But what's really bothering me is my ribs. Something's wrong."

"Take that shirt off. Let me have a look."

Balum unbuttoned his shirt and pulled it aside. His chest was swollen, etched with fresh scars, and around the scars was a puzzlework of green and yellow bruises.

"How'd all this happen, if you don't mind my asking?"

"I jumped off a two-story building onto a one-story building, broke through the roof, landed on the floor."

The doctor nodded as if he'd heard it before. He squinted at the scar on Balum's head and turned the cast one way and another. "When was this?"

"About three weeks back."

The doctor smacked his lips. He shuffled over to the flask, took a drink, came back. He stuck his nose an inch from Balum's sternum and gently traced his finger around the scarring. Then he stepped back. "Whoever patched you up did a fine enough job, but they missed something." He aimed a finger at Balum's chest. "Probably couldn't see it, with as much blood as I imagine there was at the time, but you've got a big sliver of wood stuck in your ribs."

Balum looked down at his chest and back up. "Can you get it out?"

"Oh, I can get it out."

"Good," said Balum. "When?"

The doctor was already rummaging through a tray of knives and pliers and odd instruments more suited to butchery than medicine. He paused with a scalpel in hand, and looked back over his shoulder. "Why, right now. Unless you're in some sort of a hurry."

"Now?"

The doctor came over with the scalpel and knife, a pair of vice grips, a suturing needle and a spool of thread, all of it wobbling in his arms. He let them fall in a pile on the table where Balum sat, then started rummaging through it. The look on Balum's face gave him pause. He stopped rummaging.

"What's wrong?" he said.

"You're drunk."

The doctor nodded. "What's that got to do with anything?"

"Well how about I come by tomorrow when you're sober?"

"Why would I be sober tomorrow?" He shambled back over to his flask and took a slam and smacked his lips.

Balum watched him. "What's your name, doc?"

"Call me Butch."

"Butch?"

"I used to be a butcher. Hogs, cattle, you name it. That was 'afore I got into medicine, of course. But the name stuck."

Balum shifted on the table. He considered for a moment cutting out whatever was buried inside him his own self, and quickly abandoned the idea. "You got a steady hand, Butch?"

"Steady as she comes."

"Let's get it over with then."

The doctor talked as he worked. Mostly to distract Balum from the knife cutting through his skin and the little pincer needles clawing out the shard of wood buried between his ribs. It was idle talk, hardly worthy of attention, until the doctor came around to the events of the previous night.

"Them fellows took you hook line and sinker, they surely did."

"You saw it?" said Balum.

"I was there. Saw the whole thing, start to finish. They're good, I'll say that much."

"I don't see how he did it. I mean, I saw him shuffle. Hell, he even dropped a few cards."

"Cardsharps," said Butch. "Sleight-of-hand. First off, he wasn't drunk. I expect you figured that out already. Second, that deck was no random deck. You'll remember it was his own. He had it carefully ordered, and any show of shuffling he gave you was just that; a show." He paused a moment to hold up the four-inch long sliver of wood he'd just dug out of Balum's ribs. It was jagged and dripping in blood and behind it the doctor was bobbing his eyebrows up and down. "I expect you'll breathe a little easier with this out. Now let me sew you up."

Again he talked as he worked. He'd been an enlisted man during the War, working as a cook where he did a sight of butchering for the troops. He'd seen a lot of gambling. A lot of cons. He explained a few to Balum. The Seven Card Hustle, Three Card Monte, Coin in the Glass, the Matchbox Teaser.

"Remember this," he said. "If it seems a sure thing, it probably isn't. Often times they'll lead you right into suggesting the bet yourself. They work off greed— your own greed. Sometimes they get you riled up like that short fellow did last night. Best thing to do is walk away. There ain't no beating a con man." He tied off the last bit of thread and wiped a bloody hand across his brow. When he started for his flask, Balum sat back up.

"Hold on a minute," said Butch. He unscrewed the flask and wet a clean cloth. "This is going to burn."

It did. Balum closed his eyes and waited for Butch to quit dabbing, and when it was over he worked himself back into a sitting position.

"What about the cast?"

Butch sucked down the last of what was in the flask and shook his head. "That can wait. You need to see me again anyway."

"I do?"

"We need to keep that wound clean."

"I need to get up the road."

"Not for a week you don't. Not unless you want to risk infection."

Balum closed his eyes. He shook his head.

"I know," said Butch, "you're bored to death here." He was looking out the window where great big globs of horse turds sat steaming in fresh puddles in the street. "Nothing to do but drink and gamble and watch the dogs fight in the— Whoa!"

Balum jerked his head around. He followed the doctor's line of sight out the window, where across the street Ms. Lexie DeVries had exited the cafe. She stood there for a moment as if considering something, then turned and started her delicate path back through the mud. Her great ass swayed as she walked.

"My God," Butch mumbled. He shoved his spectacles further up his nose and bent his head back to look through them. "That is a hell of a lot of woman right there."

When Balum didn't answer, Butch turned to look at him. "Ain't she, though?"

"She is," conceded Balum.

"She's a great big ball of butter is what she is, but I'll tell you something; a man who ain't lost himself at least once between a fat woman's thighs, why, he ain't lived." The doctor looked over the top of his spectacles at Balum. "You ever been with a woman like that?"

"Not quite."

"Well," said Butch. "Do you want to live, or don't you?"

Balum leaned over to catch sight of her as she disappeared through the hotel door. "I don't know if it would be wise," he said, motioning to his chest, "what with my condition and all."

"Ha!" Butch reared back with his eyes wild and laughing. "No sir! No it would not. She'd crush those ribs of yours, by golly. You stay away; Doctor's orders." He pushed his spectacles back up his nose and let out another wild guffaw.

7

On the floor of his room, Balum disassembled the Winchester. He cleaned the pieces as he went, polished them, then reassembled the weapon and sighted down the barrel. At each shot of pain he would freeze and look down, half-expecting to see blood staining his shirt, but Butch had operated with a steady hand, and the stitches held.

He went through the entire process again with the revolver, but when he finished it was without the same satisfaction that the rifle had given him. He thumbed back the hammer. Eased it down again. He tried drawing a few times; drawing and leveling and holstering it again. The same set of motions he'd practiced as a young man in the Belén jail, with Kellen watching, guiding, advising.

He dropped it in its holster a final time and stood there blinking with his eyes unfocused. It was a damn good gun. Nothing wrong with it. It just wasn't the Dragoon.

At the edge of town he gave the liveryman three day's advance pay, then saddled and bridled the roan and led it into the street. The horse hadn't spent even a full day stabled, but when Balum took to the saddle it acted like it hadn't seen freedom in a year. To hold it to a walk was a small-scale battle, but he managed, one-handing the reins and wincing through clenched teeth.

He rode west over the same ground he'd ridden in on. Mostly flat. Small rocks, clumps of tuft grass. He covered two miles and turned around and came back with his eyes scouring every rise and fall and not finding the type of cover that would conceal a horse. To any of the eastern dandies traveling west by train, there wasn't enough cover to hide a field mouse. But Balum wasn't a dandy. Years in Apache country had honed his eye. Where a tenderfoot might see empty, broken country, Balum saw a dozen places where a man could position himself just right so as to become invisible.

But aside from Apaches, there were few men that could do such a thing. If Sheriff Pickens was one of them, Balum didn't know. And he didn't fancy finding out the hard way. He set his hand to the butt of his gun and swore. He wanted his Dragoon. Needed it, rather. The Colt just didn't do it; it didn't have the right weight, the right feel, and those two factors could mean the difference between living and dying.

He considered this fact as he rode back to town. After he'd stabled the roan, he still had no solution.

He rambled through ankle-deep mud to the jailhouse and found Sheriff Pickens in the same pose as in the morning; feet up on the desk, hands folded behind his head.

"Tough job you've got here, Sheriff."

"Don't get smart with me. I keep a peaceful enough town and if I want to put my feet up a minute, by God, I will. Now what do you want?"

"Just what you said; to keep the peace."

Pickens narrowed an eye. "If you're talking about that business with whoever's riding behind you, that's your own problem."

"And if you don't do something about it, it'll be yours as well."

"Like hell. You say you want me to lock them up. Alright then; on what charge?"

"I already told you, I don't give a damn what charge you use. Just put them away before they turn your town into a shooting gallery."

The sheriff kicked his feet down and set his elbows over the desk. He leaned on them and studied Balum. After a while he nodded. "You want to be kept safe, is that it?"

"That's right. Me, and a young couple a ways up the trail."

"And that means locking someone up."

"Exactly."

"Alright." Pickens bobbed his head at the two empty cells. "Get in."

Balum followed the look, then turned back at the sheriff who was resting on two bony elbows over the desktop.

"Huh?"

"Go on, get in. I'll keep you locked up as long as you'd like. Nice and safe. You just tell me when you want out."

Balum eyed the sheriff back, but the old man only stuck his lower lip out and held his eyes steady. A damn fool is what he was. Balum nearly told him so, but instead he turned on one foot and walked to the door. He pulled it open and paused, then looked back over his shoulder. "I'll come get you in the morning, before first light. Be ready."

Before the sheriff could answer, Balum stepped out the door and smacked it closed behind him.

The day had drifted into evening, and though he hadn't had a bite to eat through all of it, he wasn't hungry. The hangover hadn't quite left him, and whatever was gnawing at his belly wasn't hunger anyway. Nerves, more like it. Orneriness. There was one thing that could go a long way to ease his constitution, and he found it at the general store for twenty-five cents a pouch.

He walked back to the hotel and around to the veranda where he tore it open and bit off a plug. He rolled it into his cheek and pulled the rocker around to where he could see both the jail and the western edge of town, and he sat down. He crossed one boot over another.

In short order, an ease came over him. A calming of the mind. He spat over the porch rail and watched the shadows creep over town. He watched two dogs fight over something, the nature of which he could not fathom, and he watched a wagon get mired down in the muddied lane and be pulled free by a single box-headed ox that held more stubbornness in its head than an inbred donkey.

He kept watch over all of it, spitting over the veranda and listening to the creak of the rocker beneath him. Before the sun dropped over the horizon the jailhouse door opened, and Old Man Pickens shuffled out. His knees were somewhat arthritic and his walk was an odd hobble that carried him down past Butch's office to a squat-roofed cabin at the edge of town.

Balum got out of the rocker in order to see him make the

short journey. When the sheriff completed it, Balum spat a great yellow glob into the street and grinned.

He was grinning ear to ear, spitting into the street and thinking about his plan for the morning, when Lexi DeVries appeared. The way his mind was wandering, if she hadn't said anything, he might have accidentally hit her with a gob of tobacco juice.

"I can only imagine what you're smirking about," she said.

He'd been leaning over the porch railing. He jerked upright and turned to her. She walked a few steps closer. The veranda was built three feet off the ground, and from such a height he could see right down the bust of her dress. She turned her chin up to look at him, which only gave him a better view.

"Well are you going to stand there ogling my breasts all night, or are you going to offer an apology?"

He opened his mouth, but he'd bitten off such a massive plug of chaw that to form any words was impossible. He closed it. He forced himself to look away from the great swath of cleavage and into her eyes, which were framed in silky waves of brown hair, and quite pretty.

"I should report you to the hotel manager," she said. "Or better yet, to the sheriff. He would know what to do. The idea, barging into a woman's room in the middle of the night like that. You should be ashamed of yourself."

He gave an exaggerated nod of his head and tried his best to show an expression of remorse. He turned his hand palm-up. She only placed her fist in the crease of her hip and stared back.

"I hope you can behave yourself tonight," she said. "I'll have to make sure I lock my door, or would that even do any good? Would you simply break it down and have your way with me?"

"No," he managed, and shook his head.

"I hope not," she said. "But I guess we'll see, won't we?"

She turned and walked the length of the veranda and climbed the stairs to the hotel door. The way her hips moved beneath the dress was mesmerizing. He'd seen what was under there. He'd seen it and felt it and he couldn't stop thinking about it.

She threw him a look just before stepping inside. It caught him with his eyes on her rear end. A little expression of exasperation left her, a brief little show that only allowed him more time to take in the great curves of flesh wrapped up in her fancy dress. Then she disappeared into the hotel and left him standing there with his mouth full of tobacco and his cock swelling in his trousers.

He sat back down and shook his head. The last thing he needed was for her to go to Old Man Pickens. As if the sheriff needed any more reason not to cooperate.

But she hadn't.

He spat again as he realized this. Despite her admonitions, she had not said a word to either the hotel manager or the sheriff. She certainly hadn't screamed for help last night. In fact, the way she'd looked at him just then, the way she'd given her ass an extra wiggle as she went inside...

But no. He needed to listen to the doctor's advice. The part about being careful, anyway. She would crush his ribs, sure enough. A woman like that. He'd never seen a lady carry so much weight, and so much of it in the right places. She was fatter than a prize pig, but the way she walked, the way she dressed, the way she flaunted it, he couldn't stop thinking of her.

After a while he put his finger in his lip and plucked out the plug of tobacco. He spit one last time over the railing and went inside.

On the way past her door he slowed down. He stopped. He looked at the knob. His curiosity finally got the better of him, and he put his hand over it and turned it as gently as he could.

Sure enough.

He let it back the other way and continued down the hallway to his room. It took a long time to get to sleep. He considered the ground outside of town, the lack of cover, the fact that he didn't feel comfortable with the Colt, how Sheriff Pickens wouldn't cooperate, and what he planned to do about it. It was all plenty to dwell on, but it was only harder knowing that Ms. Lexi DeVries had most definitely left her door unlocked, and was more than likely lying half-naked in her bed and craving another spanking.

8

He was up before the sun, before the first hint of light clawed its way over the horizon. Blindly in the unlit room he dressed himself. At the door he paused and put a hand to the butt of the revolver. After a moment's deliberation he turned and crossed the room and lifted the Winchester from where it rested against the wall and walked out.

It was early enough that even the dogs still slept. They lay beneath the boardwalks and in the shelter of the alleyways, and at his passing they would wake and follow him with beady untrusting eyes as he made his way past Butch's dispatch to the squat-roofed cabin at the edge of town.

He didn't knock. He leaned the Winchester against the wall and pressed gently at the door. It moved an inch, then stopped. A latch string was all that secured it. When the latch caught, he put his shoulder against the door and busted it loose from the frame. The door flew open. The cabin didn't measure any larger than a chicken coop, and when a squawk like a bird came from Sheriff Pickens' bedspace, Balum jumped at it. He reached it in two strides and caught the old man by his greasy longjohns.

"Hey, what the—"

"Shut up and get dressed."

"Balum?"

"I told you I was coming. Now get up. We're going for a ride."

In the blackness of the cabin Balum's eyes picked up nothing. His nose told him there was a bedpan close by that needed emptying, and when he let go of the sheriff's longjohns, it took only a second for his ears to distinguish the familiar scrape of metal on leather. His reaction was immediate— a kick of his foot— and the gun went clattering across the room.

He caught the old man by his hair. "Don't be a fool, Sheriff. Now like I said, get yourself dressed."

"And what about my gun? Am I to have that, or aren't I?"

"You'll get that back once we're outside."

It wasn't until they were stomping through the mud to the livery that Sheriff Pickens mustered his objections.

"Whatever you have in mind, you best forget it. What you're doing is a bald-faced infraction of the law, by God—"

Balum spun the Winchester around and slammed the butt into the sheriff's spine, which sent him toppling into the mud.

"I'll tell you what I've got in mind, so there ain't no confusion later. We're going to post up a mile outside town, you on your horse, and me in the shadows, and when Big Tom's men ride up, we're going to be there to greet them."

The sheriff was picking himself out of the mud scowling and muttering beneath his breath. He smeared his palms down his pantlegs and turned to face Balum. "I told you I'm not going to lock nobody up that ain't done nothing wrong."

"I know you did."

"So what then? What do you expect me to do?"

"Disarm them."

"Disarm them?" The sheriff flicked more mud from his hands and snorted. "Can't you do that yourself?"

"You know, you're about the poorest excuse for a sheriff I've come across. Fact is, I can't do it myself. Not alone against a group of armed men, with one arm in a cast. That's what I need you for."

"For what, to get shot?"

"Not if you're smart about it. I need you sitting up on your horse in plain sight. That will allow me to come up on them from behind."

"Then what?"

"Then we'll have them drop their weapons. That's not too much to ask now, is it, Sheriff?"

The old man snorted again. His eyes were bouncing around as if he were looking for a route of escape, but there was none. He finally settled on the Winchester in Balum's arms. He grunted. "Well that's as far as it goes," he said. "I ain't locking no one up."

"Let's get your horse saddled," said Balum. "I want to be in position before daylight."

They left town with Old Man Pickens hunched over the saddle, Balum on foot behind him with the Winchester balanced in one hand. They'd gone a mile when Balum called him to a stop.

"What?" Pickens looked around. There was nothing but tuft grass and sand, a few agave plants and scattered rocks.

"Here?"

"That's right," said Balum. "You stay where you are. I mean that. You even so much as think to turn that horse around and scamper back to town, and I'll drop you from the saddle and let the buzzards pick you clean."

Twenty yards away was a shallow cleft in front of which grew a small clump of grass. He crossed the gravel and settled onto his belly with the Winchester laid out in front of him. Sheriff Pickens squinted at him from the horse's back.

"Don't look at me," said Balum. "Keep your eyes straight ahead."

"I can't even see you," said Pickens.

"That's the idea."

The sun broke over the horizon behind them, large and glaring on the edge of the earth. It would shine right into the eyes of whoever rode in from the west, and Balum relaxed some, knowing this. He didn't bother looking down the trail; the point was to conceal himself. He simply watched the sheriff. The old man was fidgeting with his hat and grumbling to himself, and when the fidgeting and the grumbling stopped, Balum strained his ears.

The sound of riders on the trail came to him. The jangle of tack, the creak of leather saddles. Hoofbeats.

Old Man Pickens sat straighter in the saddle. The gold star on his vest wobbled like a target in a shooting gallery. He threw a look Balum's way, but judging by the way his head bounced around, he'd lost Balum's location and couldn't find it again.

Balum tightened his grip on the Winchester and waited.

The riders slowed their mounts to a walk. Where they came to rest was just inside Balum's line of view. There were four, not three, and he recognized each one. Bucky, the drunk Big Tom had left in charge of the Acropolis, along with three hired guns whom Balum had forced to prepare a string of horses when he left Tin City. They were the same men alright, the same deadbeats, except Bucky looked stone sober, and the three hired guns carried enough firepower to start a war.

When they came to a full stop the only sounds that remained as they studied Sheriff Pickens were the breath of their horses and the swish of their tails. The morning air carried a chill to it, but Pickens was dripping sweat like a pig roasting on a spit.

Finally Bucky piped up. "Lookie here, boys. The town sheriff come to greet us." He turned to his friends for a laugh, then cut it short and cocked his head sideways. "Something we can do for you, Mister Sheriff?"

Balum moved. He came off the ground in silence, the Winchester tucked against his shoulder, the barrel leveled over the cast.

"You can unbuckle those gunbelts and drop them," he said. He stepped forward in slow, measured paces, and kept his eye sighted down the barrel. "Go ahead and toss the rifles while you're at it."

He'd come up on their left-hand side, and if any of them decided to draw, they would have to cross over their bodies to shoot.

"There ain't no need to sit there and deliberate," he said. "I'm not going to count to five, or three, or any other number.

I'm simply gonna shoot. So let the weapons go."

They grumbled, but one by one the gunbelts smacked the dust. Rifles clattered overtop.

"What are you fixing to do?" said Bucky.

Balum didn't answer. He kept the bead of the rifle on them as he circled their backsides, looking for iron tucked in their waistbands or bulging from their jackets.

"Well?" said Bucky. "You got us unarmed. You gonna shoot us? Murder us here in the short grass? Is that how you did Big Tom in?"

Balum made the full circle and came up a few feet from Sheriff Pickens. The old man was still sweating, his eyes swirling in their sockets. He looked angry and scared all at once.

Balum caught his eye. "Your turn."

"My turn what?" Pickens growled.

"Let that gunbelt go."

The sheriff sat motionless. An odd expression came over his face. It turned from puzzlement to outrage as Balum's words sunk in. Sweat beaded on his upper lip. He wiped his knuckles across it. "Like hell," he said.

Balum kept the rifle over the four riders, but he met the sheriff's eyes with his own. "These four men aim to kill me. Taking their guns away won't do much; they could do it with their hands just as easy, considering the state I'm in. Once they finish with me, they'll ride up the trail and catch up with my friends, and they'll kill them too. I've explained that to you a couple of times now, but it hasn't seemed to have sunken into that thick skull of yours. So here's what I'm going to do," he glanced at the four riders and back at Pickens. "I'm going to walk these fellas over to the jail and put them away where they can't cause any trouble. Once the doc figures I'm healed up, I'll ride on. Once I hit Cumberland, I'll send a rider back with the keys, and you fellas can go ahead and do whatever you're of a mind to."

Sheriff Pickens hadn't moved. His eyes were as large as goose eggs, and his lips were twitching, but it was a moment before he found his words. "What about me?"

"There's two cells. I'll keep you separate. Nice and safe, just like you said."

"You mean to say you aim to lock me up?"

Balum swung the barrel around. He centered it on the sheriff's chest, and there it stayed.

"That's right. Now drop the gunbelt."

Pickens' hands were folded over the saddle pommel. One of his eyes was twitching, and his lips were drawn tight together. He peeled them back and said through clenched teeth, "What if I don't?"

"I'll put a slug through your chest."

"That'd make you an outlaw."

"I don't give a damn what it makes me as long as it keeps my friends from being murdered. Now drop it."

9

He walked them into town on foot, Balum on Sheriff Pickens' horse, the four riderless horses trailing behind.

When they entered Inglewood whatever commerce was in progress came to a stop. The smithy quit his hammering and wandered to the front of his shop with mallet in hand. Diners came out of the cafe. The liveryman put a hand up to his eyes. They murmured and pointed while Balum directed all five men into the jailhouse with the Winchester at their backs, and when he closed the door behind him he got the distinct impression that they would still be there when he came out again.

He grabbed the keys off the desk and stuck Big Tom's men in one cell and the sheriff in another. Then he closed the gates and locked them.

"We'll kill you for this, Balum," Bucky said behind the bars.

Balum pulled the sheriff's chair out from behind the desk and slid it across the floor. He eased himself down, swung one foot over his knee, and sat facing the two cells, contemplating the men caged within.

"You were fixing to kill me for some other reason, near as

I can figure," he said. "Something bad enough to bring you clear across the desert. I'm just puzzled on what that was." He looked them over, but no one answered. "Anyone care to enlighten me?"

"You killed Big Tom," said Bucky.

"To be accurate, Valeria killed him. Either way, he's dead."

"A man's entitled to his revenge, ain't he?"

Balum set his free hand over his cast and tapped it. He thought about that a while. Then he said, "I don't buy it."

"Don't buy what?" said Bucky.

"Revenge. Big Tom was your boss, and he was a bad one. A bully. A cheat. I'd lay a bet you're half glad he's dead."

"What about Ben?" The man who voiced the question was seated on the bench at the back of the cell. He was young, but the lines etched around his eyes and mouth were hard and deep. Lines of an angry man.

"Ben who?" said Balum.

"Ben Fletcher."

The image of the man flashed through Balum's memory. The shootout in Bette's Creek, Fletcher's bullet catching the barrel of the Dragoon. "What about him?"

"He was my brother. Whoever killed him ain't gonna find no peace until he's dead and buried."

Balum looked the young man in the eye. "I killed him."

The man stood. He walked to the bars. "I seen his body. There was two bullets in his chest and one in his head, and he didn't have no gun on him. That ain't a fair fight, that's murder. And I'm gonna kill you for that."

"What's your name?" said Balum.

"Andy."

"It was a fair fight, Andy."

"Bullshit. I ain't never seen anyone faster on the draw than my brother. Except for me, maybe."

"That's because you haven't seen much. You're young. You ain't been nowhere but whatever hillbilly town you came from."

"He didn't have no gun on him!"

"He did," said Balum. "He had this one." He uncrossed his legs and stood up and snuck the Colt Army revolver from its holster. He held it up and turned it so Andy Fletcher could get a good look. "I imagine you recognize it. Your brother and I exchanged a few shots, and one of them caught my Dragoon. Put it out of commission. He thought I was unarmed, and he drew on me. He didn't know I had another revolver stuck in my waistband. Truth is, he wasn't as fast as you think. After I killed him I took his gun. That's why you found him unarmed."

Andy Fletcher was gripping the cell bars white-knuckled and shaking his head. "I don't believe it," he said. "You're lying. He was fast. Damn fast."

"You can believe what I told you or you can make up a story, I don't give a damn which it is. I've got no grudge with you. But I'll tell you this, if you come hunting me, I'll kill you just the same as your brother."

"Don't listen to him, Andy," said Bucky. He looked at his partners, then at Sheriff Pickens, locked away by himself. "What are you going to do about this, Sheriff?"

Pickens only stared at the floor.

"Do you know who this man is?" Bucky went on. "He's a killer! He done murdered a dozen men out there in Hell Country. You heard what he done to Andy's brother; what do you think he's fixing to do to us? You believe he's gonna let us go? Hell, he ain't got no decency. Not two bit's worth. Do you know what he done in San Antonio? He had a woman hanged there. A woman!"

Balum had started to drag the chair back to the desk, and when he heard it he stopped. News about Sara Sanderson had traveled fast. "I told you I'd let you go," he said, "and I will. Once that happens, I hope you all do the smart thing and ride back to Tin City. The Acropolis is still there; someone needs to run it."

"Shit," said Bucky. "The damn whores took over. You ever hear of such a thing? Women running their own business? It's a goddamn outrage!"

More than twenty girls worked at the Acropolis. They were tough women, all of them. It made Balum smile to think of them running Bucky out of town.

He slid the chair back under the desk and patted his pocket where the keys rested. Then he tipped his hat and walked out through the door, the smile still on his face.

10

Just as he'd figured, no one had moved. The smithy's mallet still dangled from his hand. On the cafe porch were gathered a little group of spectators. Even the street dogs stood with their ears perked.

He ignored them all the way to the doctor's office.

When he stepped through the door he found Butch laying on his back on the inspection table. The flask was resting in his hand. He turned his head at Balum and blinked.

"I need this cast off," said Balum, raising his arm.

"I'll warn you, friend, I'm fairly drunk."

"Too drunk to take a cast off?"

"Maybe," said Butch. He pushed himself into a sitting position. "I'm drunk enough to start seeing things. That's why I laid down." He rubbed his eyes. "I swear I saw you ride into town with Old Man Pickens at the end of a rifle. Him and four others."

"You ain't seeing things."

"No?"

"He's sitting in a cell right now, and he'll be there when I'm gone."

Butch raised his eyebrows. "I guess I ain't as drunk as I

thought, then." He unscrewed the cap and tipped the flask back and sucked down a great long guzzle. Then he held it out and gave it a wiggle.

"Hell, why not," said Balum.

His first sip was speculative, not knowing what sort of poison the flask might contain, but when the first drops ran down his throat, the worry that it might be on the same level as Shane Carly's swill vanished. Turned out it was rum, and it was damn good. He took a few more swallows while the doctor started the saw back and forth.

"I guess I'm going to have to pry it out of you," said Butch, flinging the broken pieces of homemade cast aside and reaching out for the flask.

"Pry what out?"

"What do you mean pry what out? Which one of us is drunk anyway?" He waved an arm in the general direction of the jailhouse. "Old Man Pickens and them other fellas. What's the story? A man don't just lock the town sheriff away in his own jail and wander down the street like it was any given Tuesday. What did he do?"

"Call it dereliction of duty."

Butch was prodding Balum's arm around the site of the break. He stopped. "What's that mean?"

"Those four men," said Balum, "followed me here from Tin City. They aim to kill me. After me, I reckon they'll kill my friends. I explained that to Pickens several times, but he wouldn't lock them up. As far as he'd go was to disarm them."

"Four healthy men against one don't need guns," said Butch. "Especially when the fella's ribs are banged up and his arm is fresh off a break."

"That's what I told him."

"I guess he didn't listen."

"No."

Butch turned the arm over and started working up the other side, probing, inspecting, checking how the bones had set. "Old Man Pickens ain't worth the money off a collection plate," he said after a while. "Say, why do them fellas want to see you dead?"

Balum reached his free hand out for the flask. The doctor raised it up and Balum threw back a slug, and thought on this. "There's one of them," he said, "that's out for pure revenge. I killed his brother, and this kid don't figure how it could have been a fair fight. As far as the others, that's got me stumped."

"How's that?"

"The one, Bucky, he's a drunk. The others are hired guns. The man that hired them is lying dead along with the rest of his gang, and those four sitting in that jail cell should count themselves lucky they're not among them. Why they picked up and rode after me, I can't figure."

"Their boss—"

"Men like that don't hold any allegiance. They'll hire their guns out, and when the money dries up, so do they."

"So what then?"

Balum tipped the flask back. The last of the rum cut a line of fire down his throat, and he breathed in sharply through his nose and set the flask down beside him. "I'll have to think on that." He looked at his arm, free of the cast. It was somewhat bruised, but less so than his ribs. "Do I got a working arm here?"

"You will soon enough. Whoever set that knew what they were doing. Just don't go and punch nobody."

"How about my ribs?"

"They're coming along."

Balum eased himself off the inspection table. His feet landed solid on the ground and his head floated somewhere above him. Effects of the rum.

"What do I owe you for your doctoring?"

"Couple of drinks yonder'll do me." He bobbed his head in the direction of the saloon. "That suit you?"

"You're damn right it suits me. I'll see you there tonight."

The rum in his belly sat hot, and when he walked into the street where the sun shone, it burned hotter. He stood a minute soaking it in, then made his way to the cafe. Six eggs, five slabs of bacon, two bowls of grits and three cups of coffee later, he felt sobriety wash back over him. He flagged the cook over.

"Fix me five plates of grub."

The cook looked out the window to where the jail sat. "For them?"

"Aye."

The cook fiddled with his apron. He had thirty questions boiling in his head, Balum could see them stewing, but he didn't ask even one. He let his apron go and drifted back to the kitchen.

When Balum left, it was with five plates of food balanced over his arms. He came down the cafe porch like a carnival act, and when the street dogs got wind of what he was carrying they came running and barking and nipping at his heels. He kicked them away. He swore. The plates wobbled, and he stopped and steadied them and swore again. It wasn't until he reached the jailhouse door that he realized he had no way of opening it. He stood there a moment staring at it while the dogs scrambled around his ankles, and when he turned back around it was directly into the path of Ms. Lexi DeVries.

She wore a different dress but it concealed no more of her than the previous one had. A jiggling swath of cleavage steered his eyes down her neck line, and she caught the look before he could stop himself.

"Ma'am," he said. His arms were beginning to ache. "I'd be obliged if you would lend me a hand."

"Lend you a hand?"

"Yes, ma'am."

She crossed her arms beneath her bosom, which heaved her tits up. Again his eyes flashed to them, and in his mind he swore he'd not drop his gaze again.

"You have some nerve," she said. She uncrossed her arms, her breasts rippled, and his eyes dropped.

Damnit. He raised them.

"Nerve?" he managed.

"Not only have you not seen fit to apologize, but you have the gall to start asking for favors."

"Look, about the other night—"

"Oh no you don't. Not here. I'll not accept an apology in the middle of the street with a pack of wild dogs swirling around us. If you've found the decency to apologize, you can find me in my room tonight. You clearly know which one it is."

"Yes, ma'am." His arms and shoulders were screaming; the plates weighed two tons on his outstretched arms. "I'll come by this evening and offer you a formal apology."

"You promise?"

"Yes, ma'am, I promise."

"Good." She shifted her weight slightly. All hips and thighs and succulent curves.

"Now if you could just do me one small favor and open this door, I'd kindly appreciate it."

She crossed her arms again, another jiggle of tits. Balum held his eyes steady. She shook her shoulders, more ripples of flesh, and he almost winced out loud, such was the strength it took to keep his eyeballs locked forward.

She let a little huff through her nose and stepped past him and swung the door open.

"Thank you."

"I'll see you tonight."

"Yes, ma'am," he said, and she shut the door behind him.

11

That evening he found Butch seated at a table near the rear wall with a glass of liquor before him.

"Take a seat, Balum."

"I thought I was buying."

"There'll be more."

He ordered rum; he'd gotten the taste for it, and when he drank it, it went down as smoothly as the doctor's had.

In the saloon were gathered a fair number; the smithy, the cook, a couple of coal stokers from the railway company. Farmers and miners. Businessmen, or what passed for such in that hovel of filth that was Inglewood. They managed to hold back their interrogations for the first round of drinks, and then the damn burst.

Balum sipped his rum and explained. He told it just as he'd told Butch, and by the time he was finished, the townsfolk were laughing and cheering and buying him drinks.

"That old bum Pickens has been loafing on the job for sixteen years," shouted the smithy. "I say we let him sit another sixteen right where he is!"

"He ain't lifted a finger since I been here," said the general store owner.

One of the coal stokers shoved through the crowd with a fistful of mugs. "Remember what he said when the train got robbed?"

"He said, 'That's the railroad's problem,'" came the answer back.

They bought him rum and they bought him whiskey, mugs of beer and a strange concoction of fermented corn. They slammed the glasses over his table faster than he could lift them off.

"Butch," Balum leaned into the doctor's ear. "I got to get going before I'm too drunk to walk."

"Going where? There ain't nowhere to go."

Balum set a hand over his jaw. He looked at the floor and back up at the doctor.

The doctor leaned in. "Tell me."

When he told him where he needed to be, and why, the doctor slapped his knee and hooted. "Balum, she ain't looking for no apology. You know that, you pussy chasing devil."

"Well, I told her—"

"Forget what you told her. What did I tell you?"

"You said a man who ain't lost himself at least once between a fat woman's thighs ain't never lived."

"Ah, shit, not that. The other part. Just look at yourself. You've got an arm that's only half-healed and a set of ribs not even that far along. Think about the state you'll find yourself in once she's done with you. You'll be stuck in Inglewood another two months on the mend. Now you keep your tuchus planted in that seat. Doctor's orders."

He started to object, but it was drowned out by the doctor

shouting for more drink, which was merrily supplied by the gathered crowd. Shots of mezcal appeared on the table. Slices of lime and chili powder. He drank them. More came. He drank those too.

He found himself at one point pissing outside in the rain, and he turned his face to the sky in drunken amazement at the appearance of stormclouds heavy over town. Then he was inside again. A set of darts in hand.

He woke on Butch's inspection table.

He set a hand over his face and swore. He lay there a minute, then swatted his hand to his trouser pockets in a panic. The jail cell keys jangled inside. He breathed again.

When he got to his feet his head was swimming. He shoved out the door and into the street, muddy and dark in the breaking dawn. He staggered past the cafe and was already inside the hotel with his knuckles raised against the door of room number one, when a smell hit him pungent enough to make him twist his head away.

He looked at himself. At his clothing, his general state. A filthy goddamn mess.

In back of the hotel was a bath area, and he grabbed up a fresh set of clothes from his room and went to it. It consisted of a feed trough filled with water and a bar of soap. He stripped down and bathed himself and stood there naked and shivering until he dried. It sobered him up some, but not enough to clear his head.

He forced himself to think anyway. An apology wasn't going to do it anymore. No, sir.

He set his hat over his head. A few beads of water trickled

down the bridge of his nose. His thoughts trundled forward like a pushcart with a broken wheel.

He snapped up a bit straighter. That was it.

He found the hotel proprietor behind the reception desk with his nose in a ledger book. The nose came up when Balum spoke.

"Let me ask you something," he said. "That Ms. DeVries in room one. I guess her wagon is broke down somewhere outside town."

"That's right."

"Whereabouts?"

"Just over the rise, less than a mile," the man pointed.

"Would you tear me off a piece of paper and allow me that pen a minute?"

He scrawled the note and signed it and folded it in half. The proprietor took it and set it beside the ledgerbook and patted it once like it was an invitation to a royal wedding.

"You see she gets that as soon as she wakes."

"Of course."

In the street again he followed the sound of the smithy clanking away at his anvil. The shop doors were open, a fire raged in the kiln.

"You're up early," the blacksmith paused mid-strike. "Figured after last night you'd need two days to recover."

"I need three," said Balum. Around the shop lay instruments of all shapes and sizes. "If I need to borrow some tools later, would that be alright?"

"Anything for the town hero."

He made his way out of town on foot; his stomach

wouldn't handle a ride in the saddle. A few dogs followed him. They barked until he crossed the tracks, then lost interest and trotted back to town.

The wagon sat forlorn amongst the weeds. Crooked. From a distance he could see there was something wrong with the rear bolster, but that wasn't what caught his attention. It was the wheel ruts going in the opposite direction that made him stop. They were somewhat washed out by rain, but they'd been cut deep, and he squatted down and ran a finger along one of the lines.

It didn't matter how hungover he was, a lifetime in wild country had attuned his eyes and ears to the land around him. He could read sign as good as an Apache, even better in some cases.

There were no cattle tracks around, so this was no chuck wagon. Besides, there was more than one wagon. A whole caravan. There were no footprints with it, which ruled out settlers; they always had children running along beside. Anything meant for commerce would have been shipped on the rails.

He stood back up and looked around. His mind was clouded and his belly kept flipping over, but after a while he put it together. Samuel Kingston. Barney Harrington. The carnival act.

They would be nearing Cumberland soon, the largest town from San Antonio to Denver. He wondered how long they would stay. If they would still be there when he arrived. He set his hand over the butt of the Colt and let his mind wander into dark avenues, half-baked plans, each one muddled by last night's debauchery. Then he let it go and walked to the rear of the wagon.

The U-bolt had come unattached from the rear bolster, which had started a crack that had grown until the bolster snapped. It wasn't a full break; a new U-bolt and a few iron supports would fix it. An easy enough job.

The blacksmith was nowhere to be seen when Balum reached the shop, but all the tools he needed were lying in plain sight. He cradled them into his arms and walked back out of town, over the railroad tracks and back to the wagon. The movement did him good. His head cleared, his belly settled.

He tossed the tools beneath the wagon and shimmied himself underneath. The ground was dry. He accommodated himself on his back with his legs stretched out beneath the open sky, the underside of the wagon just a foot above his head.

He studied what was above him. How to go about it.

If the bolster had snapped all the way through, the job would be a long one, and one that would require the skills of a carpenter. But the wood was strong, and it had held, though barely. First thing would be to reinforce it with scrap iron, then attach the U-clip, then wander back to Inglewood and fill his belly with a steak and egg breakfast.

He set a piece of iron over the crack in the wood, and held a nail against it. An awkward thing to do with his left arm as weak as it was. Then he raised the hammer.

On the first swing the bolster snapped, and the wagon collapsed over him.

He dropped the hammer, which fell on his ribs, taking the wind from him. When his breath came back he tried shimmying back into the sunlight, but he couldn't move. His hips were pinned. He reached his hands out and found wood. He craned his neck around.

When the bolster broke, the rear wheel had collapsed with it. If it hadn't twisted like it had, the wagon bed would have dropped clean to the ground, and his hips would have been crushed with it. But it had only dropped halfway. Enough to pin him, enough to cause some bruising, but at least he wasn't chopped in half. Instead he was caught with his legs sticking out into the sunshine and his upper body trapped beneath the wagonbed.

He gave the boards a shove, but nothing budged. He hooked his fingers under the wood, drew his knees up, and tried bridging up with his hips, but the wagon was made from solid oak, and his efforts came to nothing.

He lay there thinking awhile. He wished he had a sip of water. A canteen full.

Not once did he call for help; Inglewood sat a mile away over a rise, and his voice wouldn't carry. When a stray dog wandered by and stuck its snout beneath the wagon, Balum swatted it away with his hat. He should have brought a plug of tobacco with him. He swore.

His best bet was to wait for the smithy to come looking for his tools. Whenever that would be.

It turned out it was mid-afternoon. He didn't hear the footsteps until they were close. He couldn't see anything, only caught the sound of grass slapping boots, and then the feet stopped.

"Afternoon," said Balum. He tapped a foot. "Seems I worked myself into a predicament."

A laugh came back. Only it wasn't the deep-barreled laugh of the blacksmith. It was high and sweet, and it belonged to Ms. Lexi DeVries.

12

"It was a chivalrous thought," she said. "I'll grant you that. But now you owe me two apologies."

Beneath the wagon Balum shook his head. She couldn't see him from the waist up, and he put both hands over his face and raked his fingers down the length of it.

"Yes, ma'am," he said, "seems I do. Look, about the other night—"

"You enjoyed yourself quite thoroughly, didn't you?"

"Ah—"

"I've hardly slept a wink these last two nights, worrying you might barge in again to have your way with me."

Balum didn't answer right away. The fact was, she was right; he had enjoyed himself. He admitted that much. But so had she, it was plain enough.

"I'm sorry I busted into your room and tossed you around. There you go. Now about this wagon, I aimed to have fixed it by now, but as you can see that plan went sideways on me."

"I see that."

"If you don't mind, I could use a hand."

"Could you?" she laughed.

"This might seem real funny, Ms. DeVries, but I've had

enough of it. About one inch's worth of room is all I need."

"What do you expect me to do, lift the wagon?"

He tapped a foot again. "One inch is all."

A swishing of her skirts sounded. Then a lady-like grunt.

"Why, I can't lift this."

"Could you try again?"

"Certainly not."

He swore softly under his breath. "I guess you'll have to go back to town and bring some help back."

"Are you sure you can't just squeeze through?"

"I'm pinned pretty bad."

"What if I help pull you?"

"Pull me?"

"Here," she said.

Another rustle of skirts. He turned his head sideways to try to make out what she was doing, and when he felt the heat of her thighs against his knees, he stiffened. She'd knelt between his legs. She took hold of his waist, fingers at his belt, and gave a tug.

It was useless; he went nowhere. She made a show of tugging more, rocking back and forth, until he felt something soft graze his crotch.

He swallowed. He couldn't see her, but in his mind he could picture her position. She was kneeling between his legs, bent over him, her giant breasts swaying and occasionally brushing against him. Almost involuntarily, he brought his legs closer together into the soft flesh of her hips. His cock engorged at the feel of her.

She was still swaying and rocking and giving off cute little grunts that did nothing to free him from the wagon, but went a long ways to turning his shaft as hard as the wagon axle. The harder she pulled, the more she leaned, until his cock was wedged between her breasts, her cleavage running up and down the length of it.

Suddenly she stopped.

"Oh my," she said. She leaned back. "Mr. Balum." She made a tsk sound. "Is this your way of offering me a decent apology?"

"Ma'am?" he stuttered. His breath was coming hard beneath the wagon. He couldn't think straight.

"I guess in that case I'll accept it."

Her hand landed on his knee. She ran it up his thigh and over the bulge in his pants. She massaged it, squeezed it, then unbuckled his belt and unbuttoned his trousers and pulled his dick into the fresh afternoon air.

The warmth of the sun hit him, then the warmth of her mouth. Balum's legs buckled. He clamped his knees tight against her and stared at the dark oak boards that made up the base of the wagon bed. She was sucking and slobbering and stroking his cock, tickling his balls, cupping them in her fingers, and he closed his eyes and let himself sink into it.

She pulled her mouth away. A gust of air blew against his dick. He twisted his neck around to try to see what she was doing, where she'd gone, when he heard the rustle of fabric. He stretched his neck out farther. He could see grass, dirt, a lady's boot. He was looking at it when her dress came tumbling down. She stepped out of it and turned around and repositioned her feet on either side of his thighs.

Balum gulped. Her hand slunk across his bare hip, searching for his cock, and when she found it she stood it upright and lowered herself onto him.

His cock sank into a sea of warmth, incredibly hot, dripping wet. She lowered herself until her ass was flush against him, then let out a moan, loud enough that Balum half-expected the stray dogs in town to howl back.

She was turned around, facing the grasslands, her hands braced on his knees. She started with a slow smooth pistoning motion over him, her moaning timed with each thrust. He wanted to grab her by the hips, slam her up and down in his own rhythm, but his hands only ran into the wagon boards. He wanted to thrust with his hips, but he had no range of motion. A torturous pleasure is what it was. He put his hands to his face and squeezed his temples and heard his own grunts tumble from his throat.

His ears still worked. Beneath her moans they picked up the wet sluicing of his cock impaling her dripping cunt, the slaps of her ass cheeks against his skin. She slammed herself down harder each time, faster each time, until suddenly she stopped and squatted with his cock buried inside her, and began to rock.

He gripped his face in his hands. Cramps ran up both of his legs. Cramps in his toes. His cock throbbed inside her, swollen, and when she let out a high squeal and a full-body shiver, he exploded inside her in a rush of hot cum.

She didn't move. Not immediately. All her weight rested on him, heavy, almost crushing. Hot thighs, wet cunt. He was still hard, and after a moment's rest she leveraged herself with her hands on his knees and rode him yet again. She gave him a dozen smooth pumps and came again, loud and long, her thighs squeezing him like a winch crank.

The sensation of warm air and hot sun hit him again when she dismounted. Skirts rustling, a snap of shoulder straps. She finished dressing and knelt again and pulled his trousers back up. She buttoned them, buckled his belt. She gave him a pat on the hip.

"Apology accepted," she said, and turned and left him half-conscious beneath the wagon.

13

When the townsfolk arrived hauling with them blocks and prybars and lengths of rope, Lexi DeVries was not among them. They jacked the wagon up and pulled him out, and when his head cleared the boards, a great circle of grins was there to greet him.

They joked and ragged him, the laughter rising and falling and rising again while they repaired the broken bolster. On reinforced underpinnings they drove the wagon back to town. A team of two slack-ribbed horses pulled it. They braked in front of the saloon and pleaded for Balum to join them for one more night of vice, but he only smiled and raised a hand and walked on back to the hotel.

The day had drifted by. In the last of its light he pulled the rocker around on the veranda and bit off a wad of chaw off and stared out at nothing. He spit twice and rocked, and realized with growing satisfaction that his mind had cleared. It was the type of clarity that came upon a man in those brief moments after a good humping, and he had Lexi DeVries to thank for that. He spat once more over the railing and took advantage of it.

First the carnival act. They would be three or four days up

the road and closing in on Cumberland. A town that large would keep them busy for a week. Enough time for Balum to reach them, study them, learn the secrets to their scams. Then rectify things.

He worked the chaw to his other cheek and spat. As far as Andy Fletcher went, Balum wasn't worried. The young man wasn't going to shoot him in the back. What he wanted was a showdown. Vengeance for his brother. He would want people to see it, and there was no talking him out of it. The fool was hellbent on chasing death, and a sorry thing it was, for he'd find it at the end of Balum's gun. He pitied the boy, but no more than he pitied many a fool who took up a gun against another man.

It was that damn fool Bucky and those other two that Balum couldn't figure out. What were they in it for? Not revenge, not for Big Tom. They weren't out hunting a reputation either.

Night had settled in. The rocker squeaked beneath him. He spat again and went over everything he knew of them. It wasn't much. Hell, they seemed to know more of him than he did of them.

He planted his foot on the porch boards, and the creak of the rocker stopped. If they knew about Sara Sanderson, they would know about Buford Bell. They would have heard about the five-thousand dollars in reward money. What they wouldn't know was that Caleb took a third, Joe took a third, and his own third was safely up the road and out of reach.

He stood and ripped the gob of chaw out of his lip and marched across the street.

He found Old Man Pickens dozing in his cell, the other four sitting around staring at each other. All five heads turned at Balum's entrance.

He walked to the bars and looked them over. A bunch of bums. He singled out the young man with the angry lines etched into his face.

"Andy," he said, "I explained it to you once, but I'll lay it out for you again, just to be fair. Your brother had it coming. I shot him in a fair fight, and I'll shoot you just the same if you're dumb enough to come hunting me. So let it go. As for you other idiots, you're chasing money that isn't there."

Bucky and the other two sat up straighter.

"You heard about a pile of bounty money and you think it'll be easy pickings to take it from me."

No one said anything. Bucky's eyes bounced to his friends and settled on Balum again. It was admission enough.

"Not only was that money split three ways, but my third is gone. Up the road." He made a motion like flinging a handful of dust to the wind.

"Bullshit," said Bucky.

"It's true. You give a man like me a thousand dollars and expect me to pass through five or six towns full of women and whiskey and hands of poker and somehow come out the other side with it all, you're a fool. I did the smart thing and sent it on ahead. So when you fellas get out, why don't you do the smart thing as well."

"What's that?" said Bucky.

"Go back to where you came from. If you don't like Tin City, go somewhere else. Just don't let me find you on my trail."

He turned and crossed the jailhouse floor. He was almost through the door when Sheriff Pickens shouted.

"What about me?"

Balum turned around. "What about you?"

"You ain't gonna give me no smart-aleck advice?"

"I would, but I don't think it'd do a lick of good."

"Why's that?"

"For sixteen years you've been loafing around with your feet up on the desk. You've taken pay for a job you've never done. Folks in this town are sick of you. Once you get out of here you'll have your hands full trying to talk your way out of a hanging party. Good luck to that." He let the door slam closed behind him.

The street was dark, the mud still thick, and Balum sloshed through it to the doctor's office. The sign on the door said closed, but Butch opened at the first knock. Sober.

"Something wrong, Balum?"

"I plan on riding out tomorrow morning. I just want to know if I'm in any shape to do it."

Butch slipped his spectacles from his shirt pocket and motioned to the inspection table. He studied Balum's head wound first, arm second, ribs last. When he was done he pocketed the spectacles and shrugged.

"What you need to worry about is infection. Those stitches need to come out, and if it ain't done right, gangrene will set in. Believe me, you don't want that."

"I don't want to sit around Inglewood any longer either."

"What's got your knickers bunched up all the sudden?"

Balum told him about the tracks outside of town. About the carnival.

"Alright," said Butch. "Saying you catch up with them in Cumberland. Then what?"

Balum was buttoning his shirt back up. His fingers slowed, and he narrowed his eyes.

"So they robbed you," said Butch. "They gave you the hustle and you fell for it. So what? You ain't gonna kill them; they don't wear guns, and killing don't justify such a thing. You can forget about the law, too; there ain't no proving you been swindled. What do you want, your money back?" He laughed. "It ain't gonna happen, Balum."

"It isn't right."

"No, but it don't make a lick of difference, either."

"Those fellas are going to go on up the road stealing folks' money, and that money is hard-earned. You know that as well as I do."

"True, but like I say, I don't see what you'll do about it."

"I'll think of something."

The doctor gave a dubious raise of his eyebrows.

"Before I go," Balum reached in his pocket and drew out two sets of keys, "I want you to take these."

"These for the jailhouse?"

"That's right. Give me a four day lead up the road."

"Then what?"

"Then let them out."

Butch took the keys and walked them to the sidetable where his flask leaned against a bottle of rum. "You're dead set on leaving?"

"Yes."

Butch shrugged. "I don't know. I think maybe your head's not clear. But suit yourself. It's been good to know you, Balum."

On the march back to the hotel, Balum considered the doctor's words. The fact was, he didn't know what he would do once he caught up with Samuel Kingston and his gang of conmen. Maybe Butch was right. Maybe his head wasn't clear.

He'd just passed through the hotel reception and was into the narrow hallway when the thought occurred to him. Room number one was just ahead. He tried the handle. Unlocked.

She was in the midst of changing into her nightie when he barged in. She let out a yelp and spun around. Her eyes went from frightened to curious.

She was standing only a few feet away, and Balum put a hand to her shoulder and spun her around and gave her ass a wallop with the flat of his hand that sounded like a bullwhip cracking in the small hotel room.

"Balum!"

He spanked her again. "Get up on that bed."

"And do what?" she said, feigning offence.

"Help me clear my head."

14

Balum was the first to set foot in the general store, aside from the storekeeper, who couldn't help but inquire about Old Man Pickens as he bagged up cheese and beans and slabs of salt pork and tallied them up on his notepad.

Balum made his answers vague, and when his goods were compiled he left the shopkeeper with a mouthful of unanswered questions and directed himself to the livery where he squared up with the liveryman and saddled the roan. Another set of questions came his way. He evaded them, moving from one side of the horse to the other, fiddling with the bit and bridle and a tangle of reins.

A few early-rising bystanders watched him ride out. One of them shouted something about the jail, but Balum was already past the last few buildings, and he rode out of Inglewood without a backward glance.

The roan hadn't spent more than a few days cooped up in a stall. There had been good feed and plenty of water, but the beast had a need for open country not unlike Balum did, and when they were across the tracks and onto open grassland, Balum let it choose its own pace. That pace started as a full-out canter, and stayed that way for two miles straight. By the time it slowed to a gallop, Balum was throwing glances at his shirtfront, wondering if the stitches had torn apart or if it was only a worried mind.

He rode all day without seeing another human being, nor evidence of one. Not a building or a plowed field, not even cattle grazing far from home. Only the rut tracks. He studied them as he rode, wondering what all Kingston carried in his carnival show. How many men worked with him. He wouldn't know them if he met them, and this disquieted him some. They could be young, old, good with a gun, or soft and slow. It made him distrust the world, and he felt an anger growing in his belly at this twist of reality.

On his third day out of Inglewood he stopped in a hollow of scrub oak and wedged an empty bean can in a branch. He walked out fifty paces and turned and drew and fired.

He didn't need to check his target; he knew he'd hit it the way a dog knows its way back home. But the hole in the bean can didn't change the fact that the gun felt wrong. The weight was wrong, the way it balanced in his palm was wrong. The way the hammer and trigger were spaced out from one another didn't sit right. He'd hit the can, but the can wasn't shooting back. Put an armed man in its place, and things changed. Things such as his heartbeat pummeling in his temples, sweaty palms, tunnel vision. He'd been there plenty of times before. He'd lived it, seen it. When two men faced each other with guns drawn, there was rarely room for error.

On a whim he pulled the pocket watch from his pocket and threw it skyward. It went flipping end-over-end and caught the sunlight briefly, just before a bullet smashed it into a thousand raining pieces.

The roan had been grazing, but now it stood watching him, ears pricked.

"Don't look at me, bud," he shoved the Colt back in his holster. "Look at our backtrail. When Butch lets those fools out, they're gonna come for us." He looked southward across the grasslands. "You can bet your saddle on that."

It was well into the evening of his fourth day traveling that he reached Cumberland. He expected lights, noise, piano music from the dancehalls. The city housed several thousand people, after all. A city that large never went completely quiet, and he knew no matter what hour he arrived that there would be a hotel waiting with an open door, a cantina if he should want it, and a hand of poker if the urge tickled him. A measured degree of liveliness is what he expected. What he found instead was unbridled revelry visible from four miles out.

Enough lanterns had been lit to double the size of Cumberland. They began where the buildings ended and stretched into an open field where an enormous tent had been pitched in the center and surrounded on all sides by rows of booths. Voices carried across the night. Laughter, squeals of children, shouts, a banjo trio, the crack of whips. He could hear women laughing and bells dinging, and he sat open-mouthed atop the roan and blinked his eyes at the glow of carnival lights winking across the plain.

He tamped the urge to ride into it, find Kingston, lasso him by the neck and drag him across town until his mustache burned off. He tamped it down but it kept rearing up, and he set the roan to a trot and focused on a plate of hot grub that was sure to be waiting somewhere in town.

The streets were vaguely familiar but oddly crowded for the hour, and it took some time orienting himself in the dark. The row of hotels he recognized easily enough. Three false-fronted buildings side-by-side. He chose the one he'd roomed in when he'd last come through, and he tied the roan out front.

The girl at reception offered an apologetic lift of her eyebrows at his request. "We're plumb out of rooms," she said. "It's the carnival; it draws folks in all the way from Crenshaw."

"Shit," he said. The girl blushed. "What about the other hotels?"

She shook her head. "It's the same everywhere."

"Where's a man supposed to sleep?"

"A lot of folks set up tents on the far side of town. There's bedspace in the livery as well, I think he charges a quarter a night."

He swore again and left her standing at the reception counter with her cheeks a tinge redder. The roan was waiting for him when he came down the boardwalk stairs. He flipped the reins off the hitch post and led it into the street still bustling with out-of-towners. He didn't fancy sleeping in the hay. A few nights in Inglewood's hotel bed was all it took to turn him soft.

The corral outside the livery looked like a rodeo ground. Horses stood bunched together hide-to-hide. Along one side of the fence ran a trough into which a boy was spooning grain from a sack slung over his shoulder. When he saw Balum he stopped spooning and wrestled the sack to the other shoulder. His eyes went to the roan.

"I can fit him in, mister."

Balum looked at the boy and at the corral packed with horseflesh. "You cram one more horse in there and the poles are gonna bust."

"I've got a stall free inside. It's the last one."

"How much?

"Fifty cents."

Balum laughed. "That come with a mare to keep him warm?"

The boy shifted the sack around. He raised the spoon and waved it in the direction of town. "Everything's pricey right now. You ain't gonna find nothing cheaper."

"Will those fifty cents get me a spot in the hay loft?"

"If you don't mind sharing it."

"With how many?"

The boy's eyes went sideways in a quick calculation. "Maybe fifteen, twenty."

"Jesus," Balum threw an arm over the saddle. Twenty snoring hillbillies. He'd be better off sleeping in a field. "All them fellas come in for the carnival?"

"That, and for the poker."

"What poker?"

"They got a tournament going on. Happens every year. They'll be playing over at the Bridgewater as soon as the carnival closes for the night."

There wasn't much to think on. His belly was screaming

for a hot plate of grub, the roan had earned himself a bag of oats, and here was a place that was open and ready to serve him. And a little poker thrown in, to boot. At least that's what he told himself. Somewhere tickling the back of his mind was the notion that in a crowd of men, each with his pockets full of money and greedy for more, he would find folks ready to take it from them. Men like Samuel Kingston and Barney Harrington.

He flipped the boy two quarter-dollars and passed him the reins, then turned on his heel and into the darkened streets of Cumberland.

15

The Bridgewater Saloon, the finest in town, could not compete on any level with the gambling houses of Denver. Not with the Silver Nest, certainly not with the Sagebrush. Balum had not expected any such opulence, but neither did he expect to enter a dimly-lit one-story saloon with low ceilings, floors slick with mud, and a pungent mix of body odor and horse dung floating everywhere.

What should have been one large room had been partitioned into two smaller rooms for the sake of the tournament. One of these was packed with every sort of table the owner could get ahold of, and circling the tables was a similarly odd collection of chairs and stools, even a few benches made by boards thrown over sawhorses. Two men went from table to table, laying out cards and chips and name pieces. Aside from these two, the room was empty.

Everyone else was gathered on the other side, including Balum, who stood sandwiched between a group of teamsters and a pack of nervous gamblers. This room was composed of a rough-sanded bar, a piano in one corner, and a small stage where three cabaret girls pranced around, flipping their skirts up and shaking their bottoms. Almost no one paid them any mind. The great bulk of men had their eyes on the tournament room, each one eyeing the setup, waiting for the tournament director to call them to order.

When the call came, they flooded in like wild hogs to a slop trough. What remained behind were the piano, the cabaret girls, and a few dozen onlookers standing on the mud-splattered floors or sitting at tables even wobblier and creakier than those in the tournament room. And Balum. He went to the bar and ordered a whiskey and a bowl of soup and listened to the director shout out the rules of play.

When the soup came he ate it, ordered another, ate that too, then turned his back to the bar and studied the crowd. First the girls. He couldn't help himself. Of the three, only one held his interest; there was something familiar about her. Then again, there was something familiar about all dancehall girls. They blended one into another, from town to town, each sporting a painted face and a serving of naked flesh, the jiggle of their bosoms the same no matter what saloon they danced in. Still, there was something particular about this one. The other two were advanced in age and had a worn out look about them. The look of a life hard-lived.

He turned away and sipped his whiskey. The tournament had started. Several men had gathered in the entrance of the second room to spectate. Of those that remained, they either drank, ate, or played poker on the rickety tables at the end of the bar. Neither Samuel Kingston nor Barney Harrington counted among them.

Whiskey in hand, Balum drifted over to watch. The buy-in was five dollars, and when he neared the table an older man with a freshly-shaven face motioned for him to sit in the one empty chair that remained.

"You can't say you don't feel the urge," the man said. "Not with what's going on in there," he jabbed a thumb toward the tournament room and smiled. "Go on, have a seat."

Balum sat. He told himself he was only there to ask a few questions, to gather news about the crooks running the carnival, but these were only excuses and he knew it. The fact was, the old man was right. He felt the urge.

He peeled five dollars from his money roll and stacked his chips into two piles, then took a quick study of his fellow gamblers while the first hand was dealt. The old man who had greeted him seemed harmless. He had an easy smile. His clothing bore the hallmarks of a working man. The youngest wore a pair of polished boots and kept shifting his eyes around. The third had all the makings of a professional gambler; the clothing, pomade in his hair, the way he rolled his chips over his knuckles. The fourth sat hunched over the table. His hair fell over his shoulders. The ends fluttered over his chips each time he moved his head. Aside from Balum, this was the only man wearing a gun, and he wore it like he meant to use it.

The first hand was a bunch of nothing. Balum traded in three cards and got three useless cards in return. He folded. The young man with the nervous eyes won the pot. Another hand was dealt.

Balum kept his mouth shut and his ears open. The racket from the piano was hardly music, and the way the cabaret girls stomped their feet they could have been a mob running from a fire. He leaned in to better hear the conversation, which mostly came from the old timer. After the first eight hands had been played, Balum had discovered that the tournament was spread out over two days, the ice cream in town was excellent no matter the flavor, and that all those at the table aside from the long-haired fellow had enjoyed a fine day at the carnival.

The information had cost him nearly two dollars. His chips were dwindling. They'd mostly gone to the young man. It wasn't that he'd gotten bad hands, in fact, aside from the first deal, he'd had some damn good hands. It was just that that young fellow's cards were better. They were better than everyone's. The whole table was losing money.

The old timer riffled the cards and dealt them, shaking his head as he went. "I guess all the luck goes to the youth nowadays."

The younger one swallowed. He made an attempt at a smile, which looked to Balum more like a sign of nerves.

When the cards were dealt, Balum lifted the corners and found a flush looking back. He set them face-down on the table. A damn good hand. All he had to do was bet correctly.

He stayed pat while others made trade-ins, and when the fancy-dressed fellow raised the pot, everyone at the table followed suit. Balum raised. The long-haired man raised. The old timer raised yet again, and when it came back around to Balum he pushed the remainder of his chips into the center of the table.

The old timer whistled. "That's too rich for me," he said. "I fold."

The fancy man folded without comment. The long-haired man snorted a couple times. His pile had been shrinking at the same rate as Balum's, and he gave his cards another look and pushed his chips forward.

Only the boy remained. His hands shook some. Or maybe they didn't. Maybe it was just the whiskey and the frustration of losing all his money that planted the impression in Balum's head. He watched the kid count out three dollars in chips and toss them in the pot.

"I'll call it," the kid said softly.

The long-haired man showed his hand first. He threw a full house over the table and flung his hair back and nearly shouted, "Beat that!"

Balum tossed his cards. He didn't say anything. He'd already lost.

All eyes at the table went from Balum's cards to the kid with the nervous eyes. He laid his hand out. A straight flush.

"Goddamnit!" The gunman stood up quickly enough to send his chair toppling backward.

The piano man stopped clanking. The girls quit stomping. At the entrance of the tournament room the spectators turned their eyes onto the small table near the bar, and in the silence that remained, the sound of the boy raking in his chips was enormous.

"Ain't no way a man gets cards that good," the long-haired man said. "Not all night, hand after hand. Someone at this table is a cheat."

"It's just beginner's luck," said the old timer. "I've lost a good deal of money as well."

"So have I," said the fancy man. It was the first he'd spoken all night.

Balum swore to himself. There was something crooked about the game, the man was right about that, but there was no telling how it had been done or who was involved, and getting into a gunfight wasn't what he had anteed up for. Not with that damn Colt revolver at his hip. If he didn't get rid of that gun soon he'd wind up dead. The realization struck him cold and hard as he watched the long-haired man's fingers twitch alongside his holster.

The clack of a shotgun racking turned everyone's eyes again, this time to the bar. A double-barreled scattergun rested over top. The aproned bartender behind it fixed both eyes on the rickety poker table.

"If one of you sonsofbitches even thinks about starting trouble over a five dollar poker game, I'll cut you down, so help me. I've been waiting four years to host this tournament, and I'll not have it ruined by a sore loser with an axe to grind." He looked each man over. The barrel hadn't moved. "So what'll it be?"

The long-haired man snorted again. His hand moved away from his holster. He narrowed an eye and set it on each of the four players, then turned and crossed the muddy floor and let the saloon door slam shut behind him.

16

"It's a pity how some men react to a bad run of cards," said the old timer. He smiled at Balum. "It's good to see you're not one of them. Now how's about you win your money back? Five more dollars is all it will cost to start. The beginner's luck this kid is running on can't last forever, you know."

Balum kept his teeth clenched tight. The five dollars sat in his pocket. He shoved his hand inside and gripped the money wad. He'd had good cards, he'd played them right, but each time he'd come up short. He wanted his money back, but more than that he wanted to win, wanted the feeling of it. That lightheaded sensation when you show your cards and see the defeat spread over the faces across the table, blood pumping in your throat as you rake the chips in.

But he didn't even know where he was going to sleep that night.

He stood up. "Let me get a whiskey," he said. "You fellas play on without me."

The bartender served it neat. Balum drank with his back resting against the bar, his elbows propped behind him. Ears attuned to the conversations around him. Eyes searching out Kingston.

He let all that finely honed attention evaporate when one of the cabaret girls took up the space beside him.

"You're Balum," she said.

It was the familiar one of the three. The good-looking one. He leaned back an inch and studied her again. Tried to place her.

"That's right," he said.

"Are you going back to that table?"

"Maybe."

"I wouldn't. Not unless you enjoy giving your money away. The older one is Rhett Hastings. The well-dressed one goes by Frank. I'm not sure who the younger one is, but he works with them."

Balum shot another look at the table, then he turned his back to them and set his empty glass on the bartop. He knew the name Rhett Hastings. It was the man Valeria had warned him about.

He leaned closer to the girl and lowered his voice. "Who was the long-haired fellow?"

"A mark. Just like you."

He realized he was scowling. He tried relaxing his face, but his jaw was set hard. He was tired of getting conned, and his trust in people was fading fast.

"Why warn me?"

"You don't remember me, do you?"

"Should I?"

She shrugged. "I remember you. I was working at the Acropolis when you and your Indian friend shot it up. It's hard to forget something like that."

He didn't disagree.

"A rumor is going around," she said, "that your Indian friend ran off into Hell Country with Valeria. Supposedly Big Tom followed. Is it true?"

"It's true."

"What happened?"

"They got away. Big Tom is dead. Him and his men."

It was as if he'd told her she'd won a carnival raffle. Her eyes widened, her face brightened up. "All of them?"

"Most, anyway. There's a few left. Turns out the girls took over the Acropolis and now they're running it. They ran Bucky and a few others out of town."

"Good!" She was practically beaming. "Bucky was always a no-good drunk. Who else is left?"

"A kid named Andy Fletcher and a couple others. Fact is, they're on my trail."

"What for?"

"They think I'm carrying a few thousand dollars on me. They're wrong, but they're too dumb to know it. As far as Fletcher goes, I killed his brother. Now the kid's all worked up about revenge."

Her face lost its spark.

"What?"

"Aren't you worried?"

"About Fletcher?" Balum spun his empty glass over the bartop. "No. Should I be?"

"Yes." Her answer came quickly and without deliberation. "Haven't you heard of him?"

"Not until a week or so ago. What about him?"

"He's killed over a dozen men in standup fights. He's fast with a gun, and people say he enjoys it. Enjoys killing, that is."

"People like to build up stories around a man," said Balum. "That's all that is."

"You're wrong," she said. "I've seen it myself."

"Seen him shoot?"

"He killed two men during the time I lived in Tin City. I saw both fights. He was the cause of both of them." She looked away as if reliving the memory. "It wasn't that they were unfair fights, it was just the way he worked them into a corner. Like he wanted it to happen."

"What happened?"

"He killed them both before they even got their guns out."

Balum stopped spinning the glass. The bartender was walking by. Without a word he stopped and poured another finger of whiskey out and continued on.

"What's your name?" said Balum.

"Meredith."

"Why are you telling me this, Meredith? About Rhett Hastings and Andy Fletcher."

"Valeria was a friend of mine. So were Kiki and Chloe. If you helped them, you deserve a favor back. The least I can do is warn you not to get swindled by Hastings over there."

"Well," Balum picked the whiskey up and tasted it and set it back down. "I appreciate it. I'll tell you what a favor would be though. You know any place a man can get a bed in this town?"

"Not with the carnival and the tournament happening in

the same week. Where are you staying now?"

"Nowhere. Just rode into town tonight, and everything's chock-full. Looks like I'll be making camp outside town."

"That won't do," she shook her head. "Didn't you say Bucky and Fletcher were on your trail?"

"Them and two others."

The pianoman skipped his fingers over the keys. He scooted the bench around and removed the cigar from his mouth and bobbed his eyebrows at Meredith.

"I've got to go on stage," she said. "I've got another hour, and then I'll be off. Wait for me— I've got a place you can lay your head. And stay away from that poker table."

Then she skipped up the stage just as the pianoman hammered his fingers into the keys.

17

Balum kept his back turned to the poker table. He fought the urge to turn around. He fought it hard. Turning around and seeing Rhett Hastings' cocky grin wouldn't end well. Not with the whiskey the barman kept topping off in his glass.

Instead he focused on what was in front of him: Meredith— legs kicking, dress fluttering, shoulders shaking. She was no Kiki or Chloe, but compared to Lexi DeVries, she could take first prize in a beauty pageant. As far as the two rough women on stage beside her, Balum hardly paid attention.

He watched them run through their set and repeat it all over again. When the pianoman started the order again for the third time, Balum lost interest. He leaned into the bartop. The barman was there, ready.

"I watch those girls dance every night and I still ain't grown tired of it." He tipped the bottle for a quick count.

"They do any more than dance?" said Balum.

"No," he corked the bottle. "It's a clean house. Dancing and flirting is all that's allowed. Although what they do on their own time is up to them." A series of exclamations came from the tournament room, and the barman looked over.

"Someone must have taken a pot."

"What's the prize?"

"For the whole thing? Five-hundred dollars."

Balum let out a soft whistle.

"You think that's a lot of cash?" said the barman. "It ain't nothing compared to Denver. In three weeks, these same folks are hosting a tournament there with a two-thousand dollar grand prize. Two-thousand. Now think on that."

"Are those three playing?" Balum tilted his head toward Rhett Hastings' table.

"In Denver? I don't know. They ain't playing in this tournament, anyway. Them three drifted in the same day the carnival came into town. In fact, the kid there, he's part of it. Works a booth. No," the barman scowled. "Them three have played at that table for three nights running, and I'll tell you what, between the three of them they've probably already pulled in five-hundred dollars. I ain't kidding."

"Why don't you run them out?"

"What for?"

"For cheats, what the hell else?"

The barman lowered his voice. "I'll admit there's something peculiar about it, the way the kid wins all the hands and the other two just keep on playing. I'd say it's a fair bet they're working together. But to call a man a cheat… why, I'd have to have something more than pure conjecture, wouldn't I? That's a serious charge to level on a man."

"It's true."

The barman shrugged. "If you can prove it, go right ahead. Meanwhile, have a drink on me. Maybe it'll ease the loss you took." He uncorked the bottle again and poured a shot and drifted down the bar to where a group of cowboys were calling for drinks.

Balum sipped. Good quality stuff. Maybe it did ease the loss, but not enough. He swung his head around, bored, and when he caught sight of Hastings grinning his stupid grin, he felt the liquor burn hotter in his gut. A couple of cowhands had filled the empty spots at the poker table. From the look of their chips, they were on their way to going broke. The kid's pile kept growing while Rhett Hastings and the one named Frank continued to lose hand after hand without seeming to tire.

Balum snatched his glass off the bartop. To hell with it. It wouldn't hurt to watch.

He caught a look from Meredith as he stepped away from the bar, but he kept on anyway. He'd gotten plenty of looks from women in his lifetime, and they'd never stopped him before.

He pulled up several feet away where a few other spectators stood watching. Rhett was dealing. Balum sipped his whiskey and narrowed his eyes and watched for any of the tricks he knew. And he knew a few. Chester was the finest gambling man he'd ever met, and the old man liked to talk poker. He had shown Balum how to force the cut, the top card peek, a false riffle shuffle. There was bottom dealing, center dealing, false overhand shuffles and flashing. A good range of gadgetry had been invented for the sole purpose of cheating, but Balum saw no mechanical holdouts or Lucky Dutchmen. He couldn't spot any sleight-of-hand at all, and that was either due to the skill of the players or the heavy pours from the barman. Maybe both.

The deal went around the table. The two cowboys watched their chips shrink. Balum focused his eyes harder. He couldn't spot a damn thing, he was too far away. Besides, what would he do if he did see something? To kill a man for cheating at cards would not get you jailed or hung, but more than likely earn you a free round of drinks. But it wasn't so easy. These three men weren't fools. The boy maybe— he was young— but Rhett and Frank knew what they were doing, and they were good at it. The fact that they had no weapons in sight didn't mean they weren't armed. A Derringer was an easy gun to conceal.

He raised his glass, but it was empty. He couldn't remember how many he'd drank. Too many.

One of the cowboys tossed his cards over the table and walked away, disgusted. Rhett Hastings looked at the few spectators gathered and presented to them a condolent face. He laid the flat of his hand out.

"There's an empty seat needs filling," he said. His eyes bounced around. "Anyone?"

No one answered.

"You there," Rhett aimed his hand at Balum. "It's high time you won your money back. Come now," he waved, "take a seat and ante up."

Balum tottered forward. His feet landed unsteadily, his boots scraped the floor. When he sat down he still had his empty glass in hand.

"Barman!" shouted Rhett. "Pour this man a whiskey.

No— better yet, bring us a bottle. I think we all deserve a drink after the thrashing we've taken."

Balum offered no comment. He fished out five dollars and slapped them on the table and watched the chips come back in return.

He was only there to learn, he told himself. To study, to listen, to figure out their hustle. It would cost him five dollars, he knew that much, but in the long run he'd get his money back. Exactly how he would do that he could figure out later.

The first five cards dealt to him he studied like an assayer studies a nugget through a lens. He looked at their faces then laid his cards on the table and hunted for markings on their backsides; blockouts or cutouts, shades and flashings. He looked for bends or crimps, but there was nothing. And he was drunk.

He picked them up again. An ace. A jack. He traded in the other three and got a jack in return. It was enough to go on.

He raised, raised again, and lost to the kid by a pair of queens.

His glass was full again. He drank it, played another hand, took another loss, watched the kid's pile of chips grow.

When his five dollars was gone he put down another five and stared at Frank's shuffle. He'd learned nothing aside from the fact that whenever Frank or Rhett dealt, the kid won. It was a sure thing. It was also a sure thing that Balum's cards would look absolutely fabulous on those deals, and apparently the cards of the cowboy seated beside him as well. The poor cowpoke was as drunk as Balum, and he bet on those hands every time. In the space of twenty minutes the boy had spent a month's wages, and when the last was squandered he stood despondent and dejected and shrank away from the table.

A man plopped into the empty seat. Long-haired, angry, the smell of gin on him.

Balum rubbed his eyes. It was the same man as before, the gunman, a good bit drunker than an hour ago. He threw five dollars onto the table and snorted.

Rhett started up with his amicable chatter.

The gunman cut him off. "Shut your goddamn trap and deal."

The chatter vanished. Frank and Rhett shared a look, the kid fidgeted with his chips. Something changed. Something nearly imperceptible, but it was there, Balum could feel it. The tournament was still in full swing in the neighboring room, customers crowded the doorway, shuffled across the muddy floor. The pianoman clanked at his keys, the girls stomped and twirled their skirts, but at the rickety little poker table the mood had shifted.

Rhett dealt. The cards he threw Balum were good, but the lesson had been learned, and Balum folded when his turn came around. The pot went to the long-haired man. A small pot.

When the deal came to Balum the long-haired man set his eyes on him much the same as Balum had set his own eyes on Rhett and Frank.

He shuffled, clumsily— his fingers numbed by whiskey— and when he set the deck out in front of Frank for the cut, the long-haired fellow kept his gaze nailed on Balum.

Frank's hands moved quickly. A blur at the corner of

Balum's eyes. Balum took up the deck. When he finished the deal he pried up the corners of his cards and found four aces sitting in a row. He blinked. He looked again.

He picked up the deck and dealt out the trade-ins, and when the betting started he bet hard and he bet heavy. All five players jumped in. Raises, more raises, chips and coins and finally banknotes fluttering overtop. The crowd grew. The piano went silent.

More than twenty dollars sat in the center of the table.

"I'm calling it," said the long-haired man. He slapped his last two dollars down and turned his head in a slow circle so that each man at the table could meet his eye.

Rhett turned his hand over. A pair of kings. He smiled good-naturedly and turned his palms up. The kid went next. He didn't show his cards, he simply inched them forward and shook his head. Frank turned up a flush of diamonds. The long-haired man leaned in closer for a better look. He seemed to approve. He turned to Balum.

"Show 'em."

Balum turned his cards over. An audible gasp wafted from the crowd.

"What the hell?" The long-haired man grabbed them and picked them up and let them drop again. He flung his own cards after them. Four queens.

Another wave of muttering ricocheted through the crowd.

"You gonna tell me you dealt yourself four aces? And me four queens?" His voice bounced off the saloon walls and died in the silence that followed.

A bolt of sobriety hit Balum. The blur left his eyes. He

eased back in his chair to put some distance between him and the long-haired gunman, now standing, and when he opened his mouth nothing but a fume of whiskey came out.

"You cheating son of a bitch."

The long-haired man slapped iron, and Balum turned and bent, his hand fumbling for the butt of the Colt which, by the design of the gun, was located a quarter of an inch from where the butt of his Dragoon would have been.

He was a deadman.

18

"Put that weapon away."

A Derringer came into view over Balum's shoulder. It was a small thing, but the hole it could put in a man was large enough. After a good look down its barrel, the long-haired man let his piece fall back in its holster.

"I'm taking this man with me," said Meredith. "You can do whatever you want, but don't follow us." She pulled Balum to his feet. Her gun stayed square on the man's chest. "If you have any sense to you, you'll quit gambling. You're three sheets to the wind and you can't tell a card cheat from an honest man." She gave Balum a shove, and the crowd parted.

Outside, the wind cut at his eyes. He gulped down a breath of air and stepped into the street. Meredith followed, her two cabaret friends right behind.

"I told you not to play anymore."

"You did," he conceded.

"Well?"

"Well now you know me. I'm a mule-headed sonofabitch, and this ain't the first time I've ignored good advice. It won't be the last, either."

It took her aback. She set her fist in her hip and studied

him.

"Either way, ma'am," he said, "I owe it to you. You saved my hide back there. You put yourself in danger and you had no reason to."

"I have plenty of reasons."

It was Balum surprised this time. "You do?"

Despite the hour, the street still bustled with people. Mostly drunk. Boisterous. Meredith gave them a wary look, then laced her hand through Balum's elbow.

"Walk with me."

They walked along the boardwalk with the two cabaret ladies in lockstep behind them like chaperones overseeing an adolescent courtship. It wasn't until they were past the last of the saloons that Meredith spoke again.

"I appreciate what you've done," she said. "Big Tom ran the Acropolis like a serfdom. He considered himself lord, the girls hardly more than slaves. He took almost everything we earned for himself, calling it a commission, and any time he or his men felt the least bit inclined, they would take liberties with us." She kept her eyes forward as she walked, her voice flat. "We might have been whores, Balum, but whores have feelings too. He treated us worse than dogs."

Her hand tightened on his elbow. He pulled it against his ribs and held it there as they walked. Whiskey burned in the back of his head. What she told him sparked the urge to crush Big Tom's head flat with his fists, but Big Tom was dead, his men too. Most of them, anyway.

"Ah," he said. It slipped from his mouth as he made the connection. "You want it finished."

"Yes. I want them dead, all of them. Bucky, Andy Fletcher, and whoever else is with them. I want to see them die."

"I'm no hired gunman, Ms. Meredith."

"No, not hired, but a gunman all the same. I saw you, remember? And not only that, I've heard stories. You killed Lance Cain. You beat him on the draw in a stand-up fight. Then there was Ned Witney, and Gus Farro, and—"

"I don't need a list."

"Well the fact is you're a gunfighter. Like it or not, you're one of the best, and the men I want dead are the men on your trail. You said it yourself, they aim to kill you. I'm not hiring you out, I'm simply keeping you alive and out of trouble so that when the moment comes, you can do what needs doing."

"There's a couple problems with that," said Balum.

"Like what?"

"Like maybe they won't follow. Maybe they'll listen to the advice I gave them and get lost."

"You know they won't. Those men are thieving imbeciles and if they suspect you have something worth stealing, they aren't likely to let it go."

She was right. As soon as Butch let them out of jail they would high-tail it for Cumberland. He knew that.

"Something else," he said. He stopped walking. He shucked the Colt from its holster and turned it sideways.

She looked down at it. "What about it?"

"It's no good."

"What's wrong with it?"

"Nothing. I mean it fires alright, it works like it should, but it's the wrong gun for me." He told her about the fight in

Bette's Creek and how he'd lost the Dragoon. "I've been wearing that gun since I was seventeen years old." He holstered the weapon and shook his head. "I want it back. Another Dragoon anyway. Only I want it converted to take cartridges."

"That's not a problem," she said. "There's a gunsmith in town. He's good, he'll get you what you want."

They had reached the outskirts of town where rows of tiny cabins had been built without any planning, resulting in a haphazard maze of crooked streets and dirty alleyways. At one of the cabins they stopped.

"You'll sleep here," she said. She turned and led him around by the elbow. The two cabaret ladies stood there smiling. He'd nearly forgotten they were there. "Balum, meet Betty and Sue Ellen. They've been kind enough to take you in."

Their smiles widened. The one named Betty was already blushing. Sue Ellen looked hungry. Very hungry, and not for food.

"Where are you sleeping?" he said to Meredith.

"Me? Why, at my own place, of course. Now get some rest. I'll come by tomorrow morning to take you to the gunsmith. Goodnight, Balum."

19

The cabin was dark, Balum drunk and tired, and when they put him to bed they doted on him more than necessary. They laid him on a straw mattress and pulled off his boots and gunbelt, piled covers overtop of him, the two of them arguing all the while.

About what, he didn't know. He couldn't make out what they were saying. He hardly knew where he was. He could feel their hands on him, the brush of their breasts against his face as they tucked him in. Whether by accident or on purpose, he hardly cared. He was asleep before they finished.

He woke in the morning with his cock as hard as a blacksmith's anvil, pressed snugly against Sue Ellen's rump. She didn't wake, and he made no movement for fear of changing that. Also, admittedly, the position wasn't so bad.

Only one small window adorned the cabin wall, and by the poor light it offered he took his bearings. Dirt floors. A cast iron stove. A table for four. Against opposite walls were placed two beds; one Betty's, the other Sue Ellen's. Both women asleep.

He had judged them to be near fifty, but in the blue light of dawn he reconsidered. Forty, perhaps. Maybe not even that old. It was hard to tell; a hard-scrabble life had a way of aging a woman, and these two had not been dealt winning hands. Yet the more he looked at them asleep in the near darkness, the more he found to his liking. They'd both kept their shape, especially Betty. Even beneath her blankets he could make out the curve of her hips and her petite waistline. And Sue Ellen, her lips full and tender, slightly parted, her nose small and her cheeks smooth. Laying there against him. Warm. Soft.

He squeezed his eyes closed. His head swam. The realization came to him that he was still drunk. The urge to lift Sue Ellen's nightgown and plunge his cock into her was overwhelming. To grab her by the hip, hold her tight, hear her moan as he drove himself into her. But those urges were fueled by whiskey, and he knew it. Besides, he couldn't recall exactly how he'd ended up in her bed in the first place, or on what terms such an arrangement had been reached. For all he knew, the two women had been kind enough to allow him a space to sleep on their floor, and at some point in the night he had crawled his way into Sue Ellen's bed in a drunken stupor and now there he was, drunk, unwashed, his cock throbbing against her ass.

In carefully measured movements he eased himself off the mattress and onto the dirt floor. He found his clothes, dressed himself. Let himself out through the door.

The cold air sobered him. It brought with it his memory. Some of it, anyway. He slapped his hand to his pocket suddenly and pulled out his roll of bills.

Forty dollars remained. He counted it again.

He stood a long time in the empty street with his eyes

unfocused and his temper rising. Not at Rhett Hastings, or Frank, or even at the kid, but at himself. What kind of a damn fool gets drunk and knowingly sits down with card cheats? What he should be focused on was buying a Colt Dragoon revolver, finding an unusually talented gunsmith who could convert it to take cartridges, then paying for the service. And with his money disappearing faster than coins out of a gypsy's palm, that had just gotten harder.

He ambled down the narrow lanes of shacks and crooked cabins and onto the edge of town. The hour was early but the town had begun to wake. Shops were opening, buggies and carriages creaked onto the streets. Some of what he saw he recognized from his last visit; the stagecoach station, the homely restaurant connected to it, the leatherworker's shop and beyond that, the jail. At Claire's Creamery he stopped. Not so long ago he had watched Joe kill a man in that very spot. Knife work. Half the town had been present, and after witnessing such an artful display of butchery, not a man among them had raised an objection to a white man dying by an Indian's blade. None wished to be next.

At the first restaurant with open doors he took a seat and ordered eggs and bacon, a bowl of grits, eight slices of toast, potatoes, gravy, homemade scrapple, and coffee to wash it all down. Wash away his hangover. He was halfway through when Meredith spotted him through the window.

She came in and sat across the table. "You were supposed to wait for me."

"I was?"

"I was going to introduce you to the gunsmith,

remember?"

"No." He forked up a slab of bacon and worked it around his jaw. "Frankly I don't. But you do, and that's just what I need right now. Pass that jam, would you?"

He ladled a mound of purple goop onto his toast and spread it with the back of the spoon.

"My god," she said, taking in the empty plates. "Do you always eat like this?"

"You live the life I have and you learn to eat. Out on the trail a man never knows when his next meal might come around."

"You're not on the trail."

"Even so," he spooned a heap of potatoes into his mouth, "pays to be cautious."

"I'm sure Betty and Sue Ellen would have fed you."

He looked at her across the stacks of plates. The look she gave back was an odd one. He chewed and swallowed and said, "What do I owe them ladies anyway? I'm a little short on cash."

"I'm sure you can work something out."

"Work something out?"

She smiled. Almost like she was hiding a laugh. "They were very kind to have taken you in. I think they find you quite fetching. Besides, there's not a hotel with an open room to be found, and do you really want to be sleeping in an open field when Bucky and Andy Fletcher catch up with you?"

Balum set his fork down. He leaned back in his chair. "How old are them ladies anyway?"

"Does it matter?"

"I guess not."

"Come on. Let's find that gunsmith."

The shop was located on the west end of town within view of the carnival. A sign over the door read CLOSED, but Balum knocked anyway. He stood with his head bowed, waiting, knocking periodically while Meredith stared down the street at the carnival grounds already packed with families and children and balloons and ice cream, the carnival barkers proclaiming in great loud shouts all the wonderful prizes waiting to be won. She tilted her chin up and raised onto the balls of her feet to get a better look.

"Isn't it exciting?" she said.

"If you like getting swindled," said Balum. From among the shouts he tried to pick out the voice of Samuel Kingston or Barney Harrington, but everything was a confusion of calls and whistles.

"What do you mean?"

"I mean they're crooks. All of them. Those three fellows from last night run in the same crowd."

"But they're just games. It's not like poker; there's no slight-of-hand. People win all the time. Why just yesterday Sue Ellen saw a man win a hat for his wife. A beautiful riding hat with pleats and feathers."

Balum turned away with a growl and rapped the door, but the place was empty and the only thing that came of it was the sign rattling against the frame.

"He's not in," said Meredith. She took him by the arm. "Come, let's have some fun while we wait. Like I say, they're just games. You'll see."

20

The perimeter of the carnival grounds was cordoned off by rope, leaving one single entrance where a ticket operator charged ten cents per entry.

When Balum saw who it was he jerked to a stop.

"What's wrong?" said Meredith.

"It's that damn kid from last night. I told you that crowd all runs together."

"Well what of it?"

The line was moving forward. Only a few families ahead of them.

Balum grumbled beneath his breath. It was the ninth or tenth time he'd grumbled that morning, and he felt like a cantankerous old man the more he did it. He fished two dimes from his pocket, then put them back. He shook his head. The little runt had taken enough of his money last night.

When they reached the booth the kid looked up from his ticket roll and his face turned a sick shade of yellow.

"Twenty cents, please," he stammered.

"Twenty cents my ass," said Balum. He reached over the booth and ripped two tickets from the roll.

"Balum!" Meredith scolded, but Balum had already set a

hand at the small of her back and was steering her into the carnival grounds.

They made their way around a stand of balloons, Meredith flashing her eyes over the booths of games and distractions, and Balum scowling like a condemned man waiting his turn in the gallows. When she saw his face she laughed.

"Are you going to frown all day?"

"They're crooks, all of 'em."

"Really? Tell me how that's crooked." She pointed to a booth where a man had set up a pyramid of wooden bottles in a 3-2-1 arrangement. "All you have to do is knock them down."

In exchange for a nickel the operator was offering three balls, three tries to knock the bottles down. He saw Meredith pointing and he shouted them over.

"It's easy!" he beamed. "Knock 'em down and win a hairpin for the lady. Five pennies is all it'll cost you. Whaddaya say, fella? You look like a man with a strong arm."

Balum took one of the dimes from his pocket. The distance from the point of throw to the shelf where the bottles were stacked was short enough a child could do it. He handed over his dime. Three balls came his way.

He picked up the first, hefted it, and threw. Bottles went toppling, but not all of them. Two wobbled on the bottom row and eventually came to a stop.

The booth operator grinned while he restacked them. "A touch off center is all it was. Go on now, have at it again."

Balum threw. Bottles toppled, others wobbled, and once again what was left were two wooden bottles standing the same as before. He turned the last ball over as if something was wrong with it. He ran his thumb along the seam but there was nothing to account for it.

"Try a little harder," goaded the operator. "Use them big muscles of yours."

Balum set his feet. He craned his arm back and flung it overhand as if he was trying to kill a bird with a stone. Bottles crashed to the ground. But there on the shelf, one single bottle remained.

"There's something wrong with this," said Balum.

"Oh, come now, Balum," said Meredith.

The operator chuckled while he scurried around collecting up the bottles. "Your lady friend knows better," he said. "Ain't nothing wrong but your aim."

"They can't be knocked over," said Balum.

"Can't be knocked over? Why, that's absurd. Anyone with a half-decent arm can knock them over. Hell, I can knock them over."

"Do it," said Balum.

The operator grinned. A small crowd had gathered, and he made a show of shaking his head and looking downcast. "Alright folks, whaddaya say we show the big fella here how easy it is?"

The crowd cheered. The operator came around to the front of the booth grinning and shrugging his shoulders. He extended the ball to the crowd as if they might inspect it, tossed it once, caught it, and toppled all six bottles with an easy throw. The crowd applauded. Balum shook his head. He was grumbling again.

"Not convinced?" chuckled the operator. He scouted the crowd, now full of families, and said to Balum, "Pick out one of these youngsters here. Any of 'em. I bet you a dollar that whoever you pick can knock all six bottles off."

Balum stopped grumbling. He narrowed an eye onto the crowd. A good dozen kids looked back eagerly.

"Go on now," shouted the operator. He was back behind the booth restacking the bottles. His voice had lost its joviality and had taken on a hostile tone. "I don't appreciate a man with a poor throwing arm making excuses, especially when they amount to allegations of tomfoolery. So pick out a youngster and bet me a dollar. Put your money where your mouth is."

Balum swept his eyes over the crowd. They couldn't all be in on it; there were too many. Besides, they all had the look of locals, right down to their bare feet and overalls. He singled out a frail-looking boy around the age of seven or eight and waved him over.

"So this is the one?" said the operator. He came around to the front of the booth, balls in hand, and looked at the boy. He smiled at the crowd, shook his head. "Picked the smallest one of the lot, he did."

Laughter followed.

"Now before this youngster here lets loose, I'll kindly ask to see your dollar."

Balum rifled a dollar from his dwindling money roll and slapped it over the booth.

The operator nodded. He passed the boy a ball. "Take your time, son. I got a dollar riding on you."

The boy looked back at his father, at the crowd watching, then turned to face the pyramid of wooden bottles. He bent his arm back. It was an awkward stance; his feet didn't shift with him, his elbow was too far forward, and when he let sail, the ball curved in a soft arc and missed the stack of bottles completely.

"Oh," the operator smacked a hand to his forehead. "Now you wouldn't count that, would you? Go on boy, have at it again."

He tossed a ball and the boy caught it in two hands. He stood there holding it, looking at his father again. His father flexed an arm. The boy grinned. He turned back to the bottles and cocked his arm in that same awkward stance of a wounded bird, and threw.

The throw was soft and seemed to take an eternity to reach the pyramid. When it did the bottles toppled, all six, and clattered to the ground. The crowd roared. The boy's father picked him up and set him over his shoulders, and Balum watched the operator snatch the dollar bill from where it lay and wink his eye as he tucked it in his pocket.

A growl started up from Balum's throat. Meredith cut it short by yanking him away.

"Don't be a sore loser, Balum."

"It doesn't add up."

She was only half-paying attention. Her eyes were on a juggler tossing three flaming sticks before a crowd of onlookers. A hat rested on the ground. As he juggled he made a plea for donations. The crowd laughed and tossed him coins.

"Are you going to tell me there's something crooked about that too?" she teased him.

"This whole place is full of crooks. Crooked men and crooked games."

"How about that one?"

He followed her arm to a pair of sawhorses over which was laid a pine log. A crowd of men had gathered in front. Behind the log, dressed in his gabardine suit, mustache slick with grease, stood Samuel Kingston.

21

He held a hammer in one hand and a nail in the other, and when he caught sight of Balum staring at him from across the carnival grounds, his words skipped a beat. He resumed quickly enough, but when Balum started across the grass with his head bent and his fists clenched, the words trailed off again.

"Balum!" Meredith grabbed his shirt but he shoved forward through the crowd and his shirt tail came untucked.

Before he reached the log, Kingston singled him out with the hammer. "Look what we have here," he announced to the crowd. "A man who can't wait to show his strength. Step right up, sir. Drive a nail flush into the log with one swing and one swing only and win yourself a prize."

"I don't want your goddamn prizes," said Balum. He stopped opposite Kingston, the log between them, the hammer a ready weapon. "I want to hear from your own mouth that you're a cheat and a liar."

He practically shouted it. Heads turned. The juggler dropped a flaming stick and the crowd swung to the nail-driving game.

"Go on, say it."

Kingston laughed. He let the hammer down and gave the crowd a knowing look. "A cheat and a liar, he says! Do you hear that, folks? Tell me, does anyone know this man?"

No one answered. No one knew him.

"Why, he must be drunk! Are you drunk, sir? You've got that look about you."

Laughter rippled around them.

"Just look at him," Kingston wiggled the hammer. "Unwashed, unshaved, his shirt untucked. Coming in here accusing me of cheating. He's lucky I'm not armed; I'd cut the drunkard down with a bullet through his heart!"

Balum swung his head from Kingston to the mass of people gathered. Strangers, all of them. And what they saw was exactly what Kingston had described: an unwashed, unshaved, incredibly hungover brute of a man with his shirt untucked.

"I might not look as flashy as this slicked-up dandy," said Balum, "but what I say is the truth. This man is a crook. A con-artist."

"What proof do you have?" came a voice from the crowd.

"Plenty," said Blum. But he didn't. All he had were stories and he knew it. He gave one. "I ran into him in Inglewood where he gave me a line about losing a pocket watch. Said it was dear to his heart, had a picture of his mother in it. He offered a reward, but he never meant to pay it. The whole thing was a scam, just like all these games are— "

"It was no scam."

The voice came from the back of the crowd. All heads turned, Balum's included.

"No scam at all."

Folks moved aside to give the speaker room. Barney Harrington emerged. He had lost the overcoat and instead wore a suit not so unlike Kingston's. He'd also received a haircut and a bath since Balum had last seen him, and these qualities lent him a fairly respectable appearance.

"I myself happened to be traveling through Inglewood last week, and I had the pleasure of running into Mr. Kingston there. He'd lost his watch, alright. Told me the whole story. Yes, he offered a reward, and a handsome one at that. Well folks, I'll tell you right now that Mr. Kingston here is as honest as they come. I found that watch and returned it to him, and he gave me one-hundred dollars for it, just as he promised."

"That's a lie," said Balum. "That watch is laying in the grass in a thousand pieces between here and Inglewood, and I know that for a fact because I shot it myself."

"Is that so?" said Kingston.

"Yes it is," said Balum.

Kingston shook his head as if mourning an unfortunate death. He pursed his lips together and let a long breath seep through his nose. With his free hand he reached into his vest pocket. From it he drew a gold-plated watch. The crowd stood frozen, silent. Somewhere far away a baby squallered, and when it quieted, Kingston opened the watch.

Tucked inside, plain for all to see, was the faded daguerreotype.

"Looks like we've got ourselves a cheat and a liar," said Kingston. "But I think it's clear which of us that is. Now, sir," he tucked the pocket watch away and aimed the hammer at Balum. "As I said before, you're lucky I'm not armed. I'd suggest you take your stories and your drunken self out of my carnival or I'll have the good sheriff of this town jail you for disorderly conduct."

Balum threw a hand up to the crowd. "Can't you all see what's going on? You can't win at these games. Not at the ring toss, the ball throw, the three card monte. Look at this here," he pointed to the log with over a hundred nails twisted and bent against it. "Drive a nail into it with one swing, he says. Each and every one of you knows how easy that is, yet no one can do it. The nail bends every time."

"You're wrong," said Kingston. "It requires an expert touch. The right angle, the right swing."

"Bullshit," said Balum. "It can't be done. There's something screwy here."

"Tell me what that is."

"I don't know what it is. Maybe there's something wrong with the log, maybe the hammer. All I know is it can't be done."

"Nonsense," Kingston scoffed. He pulled a nail from his pocket and held it to the crowd. "Observe." He set the point against the log and gave the nail a few gentle taps with the hammer until a good two inches remained protruding. Then he raised the hammer for the final blow.

"Of course he'll drill it in himself," said Balum. "Whatever the trick is, he knows it. It's us that can't sink the nail flush in one strike."

Kingston paused, the hammer suspended head-level.

"You're certain of that?"

"Damn right I am."

"You know how to swing a hammer, I take it?"

"I worked three years as a lumberjack in the forests of the Great Northwest as a young man, and I've sunk a thousand nails with one strike. But to do it right here, right now, is impossible."

Kingston raised an eyebrow at the crowd. "You see what he's trying to do? He's working me into a wager is what he's doing. And how simple would it be for him to win that bet? He could simply hit the head of the nail off center, swing too softly, turn the hammer at the last moment. There are plenty of ways to muck it up, all on purpose, all to prove something that isn't true at all."

"I could give the best swing of my life and that nail would crumple in half."

"You would swing steady? Swing true? A hard blow, no girlish swats? There are over thirty men watching right now, and I suspect they could suss out a ham-fisted swing."

"I wouldn't muck it up."

Kingston slapped the head of the hammer against his open palm. The smack echoed out over the carnival grounds. He measured Balum up and down. "I'll admit you look the type that could swing a hammer. After all, I'm a good judge of it; I've run this game for many years. I would mark you for a man who would drive that nail flush as easy as a dog finds a bone. That is, if you swing true."

"Like I say, it's impossible."

"You would be willing to wager? After all, what are a man's

accusations if he does nothing to back them up?"

"That's right," said Barney Harrington. "Let's see you back up all that talk with your wallet."

Several in the crowd agreed.

"Balum..." Meredith pulled softly at his elbow.

He shook her off. He looked at the log. All down the length of it were crumpled nails. Not one out of a hundred had been sunk flush to the head. Whatever the trick was, he didn't know it, and not knowing it meant he couldn't take advantage of it. The nail would bend.

He crammed his hand into his pocket and pulled out ten dollars and held them to the crowd. "Watch," was all he said. He smacked the bills over the log and snatched the hammer out of Kingston's hand and raised it over his head.

"Swing true now, sir, we're watching."

He swung. He swung hard and he swung true, and the nail disappeared like a toothpick into a freshly-baked cake.

Kingston reached across the log. He slipped the hammer from Balum's dumbstruck hand. "You see, folks? A good clean blow is all it takes. Now," he swung his eyes over the crowd and aimed the hammer after them. "You there, with the badge on your chest. Is that a deputy's badge?"

"It is."

"Would you be so kind as to escort this fellow away? I think we've all had enough of his antics."

The deputy sauntered through the crowd. When he reached Balum he bobbed his head in the direction of town. "Come on, bud," he said. "You've had your fun. Now let's go."

22

The Cumberland Sheriff crossed one leg over the other and reclined in his chair. In his hand he held a rolled-up newspaper. He tapped it against his leg while his eyes ran Balum over head-to-toe.

Balum stood silent. It wouldn't pay to say any more; he'd said his peace as soon as the deputy had brought him in, and it hadn't gone well. The sheriff was quite taken with the festivities taking place in his town. Just the day before he had won his wife a riding crop at the carnival— spotting the Queen in a game of Three Card Monte— and his opinion of Samuel Kingston was riding high.

Instead Balum looked around. Two deputies lounged beside the doorway. There were three cells in back, each one crammed tight, and the noise created by so many men locked together in such close quarters was an abomination.

The sheriff quit tapping his paper. "Would you all shut up?" He waved the paper at the cells as if swatting at a fly. Then he turned back to Balum. "Hosting a carnival and a poker tournament in the same week brings in good business, but it brings in plenty of trouble, too."

"I don't disagree," said Balum.

"Don't get smart with me. I know who you are. You came through here a couple months back along with an Indian and a black man."

"That's true."

"That Indian friend of yours cut a man to ribbons in the middle of the street." The sheriff pointed the newspaper at Balum, but Balum offered no change of expression. "I'll admit the man he killed had it coming. Still, I don't need that kind of trouble. Not with all this riff-raff I got to deal with," he waved the paper at the three cells.

"I'll keep quiet. You won't hear a thing from me."

"That's right I won't, because you'll be gone. I want you to ride out. Now."

There were times to argue and times to fight, and there were other times when it paid to keep your mouth shut and bob your head, and that's what Balum did.

"Don't let me catch you hanging around," said the sheriff as Balum reached the door.

Balum turned. He held the door handle in one hand. He took a good look at the sheriff and at the two deputies, faces he would need to remember, then he set his fingers to the brim of his hat and left the three of them with their jail cells full of trouble.

Meredith met him outside.

"What did he say?"

"Says he wants me gone."

"Gone?" She hurried up the street after him. "Well that won't do. That won't do at all. What about Andy Fletcher, and Bucky, and— "

"Would you quit yammering? I'm not going anywhere until I get the gun I want, and your gunsmith is the only one I'll find from here to Denver. Until then I just need a place to hole up."

"That's easy; you've already got a place."

Balum gave her a sideways glance.

"What?" she said.

"Your two cabaret friends?"

"Like I said, they're quite taken with you. They'll be more than happy to enjoy your company."

"I'll bet," he muttered.

They'd reached the gunsmith's shop. This time the sign read OPEN.

Before he knocked, Meredith set her hand over his arm. "I'll let them know you'll be staying a while longer. When you're through here, I want you to go straight there. I'll have them leave it unlocked. Once you're there, stay there. I can't afford to have you sitting in a jail cell when Big Tom's men come through."

Her jaw was set tight. Eyes narrow at the corners.

"You want them dead something awful, don't you."

"Like I told you; Big Tom treated us worse than dogs. His men were more than happy to go along with it. Yes, I want them dead. And I'm going to keep you alive until that happens."

He watched her march up the street and turn the corner. A finely-built woman. He wouldn't mind staying a few days in her quarters, but for whatever reason that was not the case. His deal had come up, and Betty and Sue Ellen were his hole cards.

The gunsmith opened on the second knock and ushered Balum into a small but perfectly-ordered workshop full of vices and ball molds, rulers and chisels and devices specific to skilled tradesmen. The order was impressive. Balum commented on it.

"A sloppy workplace makes for sloppy results," said the gunsmith. "And I don't do sloppy." He held his hand out and said his name was Tom Brown, and when Balum offered his, the gunsmith tilted his head back and looked at him again. He seemed about to make a comment, then changed his mind and said, "What is it you're interested in, Balum?"

Balum slipped the Colt Army revolver out. "Everything's moving to cartridges these days."

"It's been that way for a couple years now."

"The problem is, I've used a Dragoon all my life, and this little thing here," he shook the Colt, "doesn't have the right weight to it."

"Uh huh," said Tom Brown. "I thought that was you. A man in my line of work hears stories, and there's a number that have the name Balum attached to them. The man with the Dragoon," he added.

"People like telling stories," said Balum. "Even if they have to make them up."

"Sure," said Tom Brown. Again he seemed ready to say something, but deviated. "So what is it you want?"

"I want a Dragoon. Only I want it converted to take cartridges."

Tom Brown rubbed a hand over his chin. "I've never seen

it done, but that don't mean it ain't possible. Thing is, it's gonna cost you. You'll have to buy two guns; the Dragoon, then whatever weapon that has all the right parts in all the right sizes to convert it. And then there's the labor."

"How much are we talking?"

Tom Brown let his chin go. He spread his fingers in the air. "At least thirty. Forty more like it."

Balum emptied his pockets. He counted out his bills. Tom Brown watched. The total came to twenty-eight dollars and a few cents.

"It's all I've got, but it's yours if you'll take the job."

Tom Brown set his hand to his chin again. He didn't look at the money— he looked at Balum. "Tell me something. Them ain't just stories, are they?"

"Depends on what you've heard."

"The Belén jail? Down in Mexico?"

Balum nodded. "That was me."

"Lance Cain?"

Another nod.

"What about Ted Turnbull and Ned Witney? And how about Gus Farro, or the Bell Brothers? Did you really shoot a U.S. Marshal dead in the streets of Denver? Is all them things true?"

"They're true."

"Jesus," Tom Brown set both hands over his workbench and leaned into them. He swung his head toward Balum suddenly. "Let me ask you this. This gun you want me to build, do you plan on using it soon? Using it here?"

"I do."

"Alright then." The gunsmith opened his hands for the twenty-eight dollars. "If I get to see you in action it'll be worth eating a loss on this gun."

"How long will it take?"

"It'll take some time. Are you in a hurry?"

"Sort of. I expect the men on the receiving end of that gun to show up in a few days."

"I'll work as quick as I can. In the meantime at least you got the carnival to keep you entertained. I'd caution you not to play the games though."

"Too late," said Balum.

"They got you already, did they?"

"The pyramid throw and the nail drive."

Tom Brown offered up a grimace. "Thieves is what they are. They came through last year and fleeced me good. I got mad, of course, then after I calmed down I got curious. I got wrapped up on figuring out their hustles. They're damn good at what they do, I'll give them that. Now I go just to watch them work."

"You know how it's done?"

"The cons? Most of 'em. Take that pyramid game you lost at. How come you can't knock all six bottles down no matter how well you throw, yet that fella can do it any time he pleases?"

Balum shrugged.

"Here's how. Three of them wood bottles don't weigh nothing at all. The other three are weighted down with lead. They must weigh fifteen pounds apiece. If he puts those heavy ones on the bottom, you ain't gonna knock 'em down no matter how hard you throw. But if he sets them overtop of the light ones, why any half-assed throw will topple them."

"How about the pine log and the nails? Is it the hammer? The log? What's the trick?"

Tom Brown grinned. "It's the nails. He's got two pockets where he pulls them from. In one pocket he's got regular nails, real sharp. If he wants to drive one home, he uses one of those. In the other pocket he's got a bunch of nails that he's filed down to dull nubs. He can get them started with a couple taps, but any hard swing is going to bend them. And that's just what happens."

Balum swore.

Tom Brown was still grinning. "It's a helluva thing, ain't it? They got all kinds of tricks."

"And you know them all?"

"Well, almost. They've got a new one I ain't seen in action yet. It's called the Kingston Crackshot. It's a big wheel, as big as a man, and the word is that as a grand finale he's going to tie a man to that wheel, give it a spin, and put five bullets all around him. That'll be tomorrow night. He's selling the tickets now at fifty-cents apiece."

"You say he's going to tie a man to it?"

"Tie him up with his arms and legs spread out like the Vitruvian Man."

"What's that?"

"Leonardo da Vinci. Italian. You probably seen it drawn somewheres before. Anyway, like I say, I don't know how he'll do it. Who the heck would take that risk getting tied up there?"

"Maybe Kingston is a crackshot like he says."

"Maybe. But think on this; he might sell a hundred and fifty dollars' worth of raffle tickets, but he's got to split that money. And even if he can do it once, can he do it over and over? He sets it up in every town that's big enough to host the carnival. It just ain't worth the risk. Not of dying it ain't."

"It would have to be a fool to let himself get tied up there," Balum agreed.

"Aye. Or there's something else going on. Anyway, if you want that gun of yours, you better let me get to work. Feel free to stop in tomorrow and see how she's coming along."

23

The cabin was unlocked, dark. Balum entered and found it empty. The ladies would be at the Bridgewater Saloon, dancing and shaking their rumps for the drunks, and by the time they got back he planned to be fast asleep. In the meantime he had time to kill and nothing to kill it with.

He took a seat at the table and crammed a wad of chaw in his lip. He rolled up the sleeve of his left arm. The break was healing, but still, he wouldn't want to throw a punch with it. Absentmindedly, he set his fingers over his chest. Butch had done a damn good job, drunk or not.

At the thought of the doctor, Balum dropped his hand to the Colt. The doctor would have opened the cell by now. Somewhere on those windswept plains between Inglewood and Cumberland were four armed men riding hard and set on violence.

Balum eased his grip. The Dragoon would be ready soon. It had to be. The Colt Army revolver was his own death sentence sitting in that holster.

He got up and cracked the door and spit into the street. He stood a long time in the doorway, watching the shadows grow, listening to the cadence of the town shift from evening to night.

He couldn't make up his mind which bed to sleep in. He couldn't figure out what those ladies expected from him— or maybe he didn't want to. If he was honest with himself he couldn't say exactly what he wanted from them either. At first sight, he had ignored them. A couple of worn-out dancehall ladies. But after a few drinks he had looked again. And then in the morning, waking beside Sue Ellen, the smell of her, the feel of her plush rump nestled firmly against his crotch, it made him doubt his own judgement.

He plucked his hat off and tossed it on the table. The hell with it. He wasn't drunk now.

He pulled one blanket from each bed and arranged them on the floor, then stripped nearly naked and crawled inside. He was asleep in under a minute.

When they came home the hour was late and the cabin pitch black, and if they'd not lit a candle he would never have woken. But they did. The light caused him to roll in his blankets.

"Balum!" said Betty. "What on earth are you doing on the floor? Here, let me help you."

She pulled him up half asleep and guided him to her bed. He wore nothing but his underwear. A comment escaped Sue Ellen's mouth, and Betty giggled. He didn't catch it. He didn't much care. He hit the mattress and was out again before they'd extinguished the flame.

In the morning he woke the same as the previous. Only this time with his cock prodding Betty's warm flesh. She wore a nightie similar to what Lexi DeVries had worn, and at some point in the night Balum had turned toward her. She hadn't pushed him away. Maybe she hadn't noticed, maybe she was simply asleep and unaware.

That was a lie he was telling himself, and he knew it. What they expected from him was to mount them like a wild bull let loose among a flock of heifers and pound them until their legs quivered and their eyes rolled back in their heads. They just didn't know how to reach that end. They were older than him. Not by all that much, but enough to make them conscious of it. And not all women were as provocative as Lexi DeVries. Just the fact that they'd allowed him in, shared their bed with him, it was already more forward than most women would behave.

Balum closed his eyes. Kiki and Chloe had spoiled him. Angelique spoiled him. Hell, even Lexi DeVries would leave these two in the dust in a beauty pageant.

He looked over Betty's shoulder at Sue Ellen asleep on her bed. The light was poor. He didn't know if that helped or hurt. Then again, near any woman looks fetching when a man wakes hard as a flagpole first thing in the morning.

As careful as he could he crawled out of bed, over Betty, over to the table where he'd laid out his clothes. He dressed with his back to them. When he turned around he caught them looking. Betty snapped her eyes shut. Sue Ellen did not.

"Good morning, Balum," she smiled.

"Morning, ma'am."

"You're not planning on going out, are you? Meredith told us what happened with the sheriff."

"Well," Balum hitched his belt up. "There's something I need to check on. Something in town."

"Can it wait just a little bit? There's a couple things here that need fixing. Betty and I thought maybe, if you don't mind of course, maybe you could help out?"

"Of course," said Balum. "You two have been awfully kind letting me stay here. Least I can do is lend a hand. Now what is it you say needs fixing?"

"Oh let me show you." She pulled the covers away and lowered her feet over the side of the bed. She wore a pair of white panties and a matching white bra, nothing else. She stood up, then looked down as if surprised, and made a weak show of covering her breasts with one hand and her panties with the other.

Balum swallowed, but he didn't look away. Her breasts were larger than he had realized. She had large thighs, working thighs, and a little extra weight in her arms, but her waist still held its shape, and her skin was smooth and tight.

"Oh my," she smiled coyly, "I'm hardly dressed. How indecent of me."

"Don't worry, ma'am. It's your house, you should feel at ease in it."

"You don't mind?"

"Not at all." He said it without thinking. Hell, it was true, if he was to admit it to himself.

"Betty, help me show Balum what's wrong with this table."

Betty slid out of bed and brushed a hand over the front of

her wrinkled nightie. She didn't have the cute button nose or the full lips like Sue Ellen, but she didn't have the extra weight, either. In fact, every ounce of her was placed just to Balum's liking, and it had settled in gracefully with her age. She saw him looking, and she blushed. "I really should put something on."

"You heard him," said Sue Ellen. "He said he doesn't mind, isn't that right?"

"No ma'am," he said again.

"Now look at this," She brushed past him to the table and took one corner and shook it. The whole thing wobbled. Worse than the tables in the Bridgewater Saloon. "I think the problem is where the legs attach. The screws have come loose."

She lowered herself onto her knees, then her hands, and crawled halfway under the table and twisted her chin up. Her panties couldn't cover the expanse of skin required of them. They scrunched up into the crease of her butt, her cheeks bare and waving side-to-side while she made an inspection of the table legs.

"Yes, they're definitely loose." She crawled out and came to her feet again and hooked a thumb into the edge of her panties and adjusted them.

It didn't take more than a few minutes for Balum to tighten the table legs. A few twists with a screwdriver was all it took. When he came out from underneath the table they had another project ready.

"It started leaking a month ago." Betty was pointing to a spot in the ceiling. "We have the stucco and the laths, but neither of us can reach it."

Balum looked up. The ceiling wasn't all that high. He pulled a chair around and climbed onto it. "Just hand me up the tools and I'll get her patched up," he said.

"Be careful, Balum," said Betty. She put both hands around his calf as if to steady him. He wasn't more than a couple feet off the ground. If he fell nothing would happen, but he didn't say anything. Sue Ellen handed up the bucket and laths, and while he worked she copied Betty and put her hands around his other leg.

As he worked he noticed that their grips tightened. Their hands moved a few inches up his thighs. When he shifted his weight they hugged him against their breasts and cautioned him again to be careful.

He looked down. A mistake. What he saw were two half-naked women with their heads tilted back, breasts smashed up against his legs, the smooth white flesh of their throats bare and tantalizing beneath him. He almost dropped the trowel. He blinked hard and told himself not to look down again, but he did, several times, first at one, then at the other, the heat of their bodies burning through his pantlegs.

When he finished the stucco work and stepped down from the stool they kept their hands on him longer than needed.

"Thank you so much, Balum," Sue Ellen cooed, and gave him a hug. A tight hug. It was only natural to wrap an arm around her waist. His hand on her bare skin. The edge of her panties. The smell of her skin drilling into his head.

His cock bulged, and he wondered if he was going crazy. He slipped away from her.

"Like I say, I need to check on something. Don't you two worry, I'll be back soon enough."

"Watch out for the sheriff, Balum."

"I'll be careful." He squared his hat over his head as he stepped through the door, and left the two dancehall ladies and their hot naked flesh behind him.

24

Balum kept to the backstreets and the shaded alleyways as he made his way to Tom Brown's workshop. He kept his hat pulled low. From beneath its brim he saw neither sheriff nor deputy, and when he reached the gunsmith's shop and found it open, his breath came a little easier.

"I work fast, but I can't do miracles," Tom Brown said as he let Balum in.

"How far along are you?"

"Not very. Took me all day yesterday to track down what we need. Here's what I come up with." He motioned Balum over to the workbench where two revolvers had been disassembled and the pieces arranged over two towels. "This here is your Colt Dragoon, third model. I reckon you'll appreciate that; the first and second editions got squareback trigger guards, and from what you told me about your old one, that ain't what you want. Now over here," he pointed, "we got a Colt .45, nearly brand new. What I aim to do is put the .45 cylinder on the Dragoon. You'll be able to use the .45 Colt cartridge and, in a pinch, it'll even take the shorter .45 Schofield cartridge." He set his hands over his hips, pleased with himself.

Balum looked at the pieces laying over the towels and back at Tom Brown. "This is going to take a while."

"That's what I been telling you."

"I know it. It's just every hour that goes by I feel less comfortable about this thing," he pulled the Colt Army revolver an inch from its holster and let it fall again. "I'm liable to get myself killed if I have to use it."

Tom Brown waved him off. "That's just your mind screwing with you. Say, have you bought a raffle ticket for tonight? Just about the whole town has, me included. Everybody wants to see this crackshot business."

"No," said Balum. He told the gunsmith about the sheriff's directive to leave town. "I need to stay low, not be seen."

"So where are you hiding?"

"With a couple of them dancehall girls from the Bridgewater Saloon."

"Meredith? She's something, ain't she."

"No, the other two. Sue Ellen and Betty."

"Oh. Too bad it ain't Meredith. Them other two are a little worn around the edges." Tom Brown shrugged. "A man can't always win top prize though, can he?"

"Funny thing is," said Balum, "that's what I thought when I first saw them. But they've grown on me; a little bit each day. Clear to the point that my mind starts wandering to them if I don't keep busy."

"Uh huh," said Tom Brown. He wagged a finger. "Island Syndrome, that's what that is."

"Island Syndrome?"

"Say a man winds up shipwrecked on a desert island with no one but a beat up old hag to keep him company. First couple days, he keeps his distance. Don't want nothing to do with her. Then after a while he notices she's got a pretty smile. Good teeth, maybe. Then nice eyes. Heck, she ain't fat, she moves like a woman. You let enough time go by, that old hag turns into the fairest damsel the world has ever known, and he's following her around like a lost dog begging for a scrap of food." Tom Brown nodded at his own wisdom. "Longer you stay cooped up with them two women, the more you'll fancy them. I guarantee it."

The gunsmith had made a fine point, and Balum didn't argue. In fact his mind had drifted to Sue Ellen's pretty lips and the way Betty's nightie fell over her hips. He was wrapped up in these thoughts when a knock sounded.

He stepped to the wall behind the door and palmed the Colt. He let it go when Meredith came through.

She came in with her face flushed and her breath coming in short hard bursts. "Balum, they're here!"

"Who?"

"Bucky and Andy Fletcher and a couple of his old gunhands."

He went to the workshop window, but it gave onto an alleyway and there was nothing to see there. He swore. Butch had let them out too soon. He'd more than likely gotten drunk and lost count of the days.

"Balum, they know you're here. First place they went was the livery. They'll have seen your horse there."

He swore again.

"What are you doing here, anyway?" she said. "You were supposed to stay put in the cabin."

"Don't chide me. I need my Dragoon, and until Tom Brown fashions it up I don't fancy getting into no shooting match."

Meredith swung around. "When will that be?"

"Well," the gunsmith hesitated. "Honestly ma'am, it ain't gonna happen today."

"Tomorrow?"

"Maybe. Or maybe the day after that."

She was shaking her head and a frown was building over her eyes. "We're going to have to get you back to the cabin without being seen. Not by the sheriff, the deputies, or any of Big Tom's men."

"Where are they now?"

She flung a hand up. "They're all over! How am I supposed to keep track of them?"

"Easy now," said Balum. "We'll take the backstreets, stay off the main drag."

"There's too many of them. Someone is bound to see you"

She was right. Counting the sheriff and his deputies, there were at least seven men if not more, on the lookout for him.

"Come here," he crooked a finger at her. "I've got an idea."

"What?"

"You're about the prettiest girl in town, and the sight of you turns some heads. We've just got to turn a few more. Now get over here."

She wore a blue calico dress with buttons running up the front clear to her throat. He unlooped the first button, then the second, then continued down the line until he had exposed a heavy swath of skin. Her breasts were not large, but they weren't small either. He reached a hand down the bustline and took one in his palm and pulled it up, almost out of the dress.

"Balum!"

He pulled the other one up and she swatted him on the arm. "Shame on you."

"That's better," he stepped back. "Tom Brown, what do you think? Is she gonna take some attention off me?"

Tom Brown's eyes bulged. He looked at the floor, looked at the workbench, then snuck another look at Meredith. His cheeks had gone red and he stuttered something unintelligible.

"Yep," said Balum. "Alright then, are you ready? I want you to walk twenty paces ahead of me. I'll be right behind."

25

They went up the alleyway past the gunsmith's window and turned onto a smaller street that housed several bakeries and a coffin maker's shop. It worked just as Balum had figured it would; heads turned, eyes went as big as duck eggs. Jaws dropped.

Balum kept his head down and his hat low. He looked up every now and then to keep her in sight, then he dropped his eyes again.

Halfway across town she came out of an alleyway and onto the second-largest street in Cumberland. There was no choice but to cross it. She drew up and looked both ways, then she threw a look back over her shoulder and started across.

She had just reached the other side when two wagons traveling in opposite directions met in the street. The drivers knew each other. They pulled their teams to a stop and greeted one another from their driving benches. Meredith, somewhere on the opposite boardwalk, was lost from sight. Without her jiggling tits to distract the passersby, the attention began to settle on Balum; a tall stranger, wide in the shoulder, a gunbelt strapped to his hips, caught flat-footed in the middle of the street.

He spun right and circled the wagon and when he came around the other side he raised his head to scan the boardwalk. It wasn't a long look, just a glance. But it was long enough.

"Hey!"

It was Bucky. He was standing on the boardwalk directly between Balum and Meredith with one arm up and his finger aimed on Balum.

Balum spun. He wove through a group of carnival-goers, children carrying balloons, and onto the next block over. Bucky wouldn't shoot, not with all these people around. Besides, the fool wanted money, and for that he would want Balum alive. It was Andy Fletcher he had to watch out for.

Before he turned up the cross-street he looked back. The idiot was clomping down the boardwalk, shoving folks aside and creating a scene.

There was only one way forward, and that was up a narrow lane that ran smack into Cumberland's main drag. Balum took it at a run.

When he came to the end of the lane he slowed to a walk and stepped into the throng of people bustling down the main drag. He kept to the street, away from the boardwalk, making his way past hitch rails and watering troughs, skirting around parked buggies and strings of horses swishing their tails. With so many visitors in town the street was packed, and as long as he kept to the busiest parts, he might lose Bucky and make it through unseen.

Until he hit Claire's Creamery. The line of customers stretched clear across the street, and when he attempted to cut through them the outcries were severe enough to draw the attention of half the town.

"Hey, no cutting, mister!" shouted a chubby boy in suspenders.

"Get to the end of the line, buddy," someone further down said.

Others joined in. Mumbles and grumbles and fingers pointing. Then his name.

"Balum!"

It was spoken sharply and clearly and rose above all else, and the man who spoke it was Andy Fletcher. The young gunfighter stood some fifty yards up the street with his legs spread and his right hand inches from his holster.

Folks scattered. Women screamed, yanked their children away. The line at Claire's Creamery broke and fled to the boardwalks, to relative safety, and as Balum turned he saw among them the faces of Bucky, the Cumberland Sheriff, one of the deputies with a cigarette dangling in his lips. He spotted Rhett Hastings and Barney Harrington conspiring together outside the leatherworker's shop and, farther down, the gambler by the name of Frank. Climbing onto a hitch rail was the liveryboy hoping to get a better view. Over a hundred people stood watching, waiting, knowing that death was coming and savoring it like one of the carnival acts for which they'd ridden in from far and wide.

Andy Fletcher gave them what they wanted. "You killed my brother," he shouted loud enough to reach the carnival grounds. "Ain't no way in hell that was a fair fight. Only way you could have done it was to shoot him unarmed." He waited for the words to take effect. He enjoyed his moment, all the attention on him. "Well what'll you do now, huh? Now that you got to face a man in a fair fight?"

To answer him was foolish. Andy Fletcher had come to kill. The thing to do was draw and fire, end it already. But to draw that goddamn Colt Army revolver...

Maybe he could talk his way out. Allow time for the sheriff or one of the deputies to step in.

"I told you already, that was a fair fight," said Balum.

"Liar!"

"You don't need to do this, Andy. You can still—"

Andy's hand dropped. He was fast, there was no denying that. Meredith hadn't exaggerated his speed; his hand simply twitched, and then the gun was out and leveling. He was damn fast.

But he was no Lance Cain, and even as Balum drew he knew he had the young man beat. He knew he would clear leather sooner, knew he would cock the hammer back just a touch faster, and he knew he would get his shot off before Andy ever would. And all of that was true. It all played out just like he figured. Except for one thing.

He missed.

The Colt Army revolver weighed two pounds eleven ounces, considerably lighter than the Dragoon, which came in at four pounds two ounces. The position of the hammer varied one-sixteenth of an inch and the width of the trigger guard even less than that, but all these factors together, combined with a racing heart and sweaty palms and tunnel vision, were enough to alter Balum's shot. The bullet whistled over Andy Fletcher's left shoulder and sailed out of town as clean as when it left the barrel.

Balum's thumb went to the hammer again, but even as he cocked it back his chest tightened in expectation of the bullet that was sure to rip it open. But the bullet didn't come. The shot never came. Andy Fletcher's gun had jammed.

For a moment, nobody on Main Street breathed. Not an inhale, not an exhale. They stood witness to one man with a ready gun and another with a bullet misaligned in his cylinder. They stood witness to a pending execution. But for those anxious to see a helpless man gunned down in the street, they went home without satisfaction; Balum didn't fire. He had killed men, yes, but he was not a murderer. The difference was small but it was a difference that separated an honest man from a scoundrel, a good man from evil.

He caught the eyes of the sheriff, the deputies, Bucky, Barney, Rhett Hastings, and he slammed his gun back into his holster and took off running.

The street was clear; everyone was scrunched against the storefronts. They heard his boots hit sand, the soft jangle of spurs, and when he hooked right and vanished into the lane aside the mercantile they heard nothing but their own shuttered breath slowly return.

26

A pot with a broken handle, a dresser drawer that wouldn't close, and a door jamb that had warped and needed repair. These were the tasks Sue Ellen and Betty had laid out for Balum, and grateful he was for them, for it occupied his troubled mind.

He'd faced men in battle so many times he'd lost count. It wasn't that he had no fear— fear was there every time— it was that his confidence was enough to overpower it. He knew his ability with a gun. It was an ability born through natural inclination, one which he had honed over the years by endless hours of practice. Hours drawing, holstering, drawing again. A mountain's worth of caps and balls, a thousand pounds of powder. It had all served to keep him alive until this day, this moment, and now everything fell into question.

Halfway through the dresser repair he voiced his thoughts. He couldn't help himself; Sue Ellen and Betty were hanging around watching. If they were still half-naked maybe his mind would drift, but they had dressed themselves in proper attire to watch the Kingston Crackshot that evening.

"Balum, I don't think you have anything to worry about," said Sue Ellen. "Like you say, you've lived all your life with a different gun. You're not used to this one. You've never liked the feel of it since you first picked it up, you said so yourself."

"Still," said Balum, "I live by the gun. If I can't use it anymore it means I'll die by it too."

"Your mind is spinning. Once you have your Dragoon back, it will calm. You'll see."

Balum slid the drawer shut. He pulled it out and slid it shut again and raised his eyebrows. Betty gave a little clap.

"That's the last of the chores," he said. "You sure there isn't something for me to do while you're gone?"

"There's nothing left but to sit here and stew," said Sue Ellen. "And that's no good. Why don't you come with us?"

"I can't go out. Not with all of them looking for me."

"Of course you can. There's almost no moon tonight, the town will be pitch black, and everyone will have their eyes on the show. Besides, don't you want to see it? Why, it's incredible! He's going to shoot at a man tied to a spinning wheel!"

A grunt was all Balum offered in response. It was true, he wanted to see it. The idea of shooting at a man like that was absurd. It intrigued him.

"I haven't bought a ticket," he said.

"We can watch from a distance," said Sue Ellen.

"I can't afford to be seen."

"It's already dark; no one will notice you. Come on. Leave your gun here. It's going to start soon."

To reach the carnival grounds on the opposite side of town they circled to the north, which added nearly a quarter-mile to the trip. They reached the Kingston Crackshot just as

Samuel Kingston was making his speech to over a thousand silent spectators.

He stood on a raised platform with his face lit orange by the dozens of torches that had been set on twelve-foot poles all around. A great many more had been placed around the wheel. It was constructed on a wooden frame several feet deep. Over this frame was strung a sheet of canvas as taut as a snare drum. A great mountain of hay bales were stacked behind it, enough so that a cannonball wouldn't have penetrated, let alone a bullet. They began at the sides of the frame and rose like a fortress ten feet high and another ten deep. The wheel easily measured seven feet in diameter, but no one was yet attached.

Kingston strutted back and forth on his platform. It was the first time Balum had seen him wear a gunbelt. It looked brand new. Unused. So did the handle of the Colt .45 poking from the holster. Kingston was gesturing in great sweeping arcs of his arm and jinying up the crowd. His voice carried across the carnival grounds all the way to where Balum and the girls stood.

"I must warn you, ladies and gentlemen, that what you will witness here tonight should not be attempted by any other than myself, the single greatest crackshot in living history. The danger is too great. Too real. A man could die tonight. Is that not why you have come— to see a man risk life and limb? To face death? Would any of you do such a thing?" He pointed to a lady in the front row. "You ma'am. Would you allow yourself to be tied to that wheel, allow my assistant to spin it, and allow me to fire five bullets all around you?"

The woman blushed. She shook her head.

"She will not!" cried Kingston.

The crowd laughed.

"But I can't blame her. I expect none of you would volunteer yourselves, and not out of cowardice, but out of good sense. You are asking yourselves right now: what if he misses? Well ladies and gentlemen, allow me to introduce myself yet again in case you forgot. I am Samuel Kingston, the single greatest crackshot in living history. I never miss. I put my bullets where I want them. My assistant Frank knows this, and armed with this knowledge he has no fear. Please, a hand for Frank."

The well-dressed gambler walked into the torch light and into a crush of applause. He removed his hat and bowed, then passed the hat to one of Kingston's assistants and walked to the wheel. Four sections of rope hung from the edges. He extended all four limbs. The Vitruvian Man.

Kingston's assistants tied him wrist and ankle and bowed and walked away in the thunder of another applause. When the crowd quieted, Kingston spoke again.

"Ladies and gentlemen, not only will I fire five bullets, but I will tell you now where those bullets will land." He paused for effect. "I will put one bullet between his legs, two more at the elbows, and I shall place a bullet on either side of his head."

A few gasps went up.

"Frank, are you ready?"

"Ready, sir," Frank said from the wheel.

"Ladies and gentlemen, are you ready?"

Someone in the crowd shouted, "We're ready!"

"Spin him, boys!"

Betty clutched Balum's arm tighter. They stood on a small knoll at the back of the crowd, but the light from the torches was plentiful enough to make out the gleam on the barrel of the Colt .45 when Samuel Kingston pulled it out.

He made the move quickly, yet the draw wasn't quick. His elbow came back too far, swayed oddly out from his body, the barrel swung too high, then dropped down again.

To Balum's eye, an eye that had seen a lifetime's worth of revolver shots, it seemed he was sure to miss. The movement was stiff, hacky, yet the crack of the gunshot was clear enough.

As one solid mass, the crowd leaned forward. Betty leaned forward. Sue Ellen leaned forward. Balum narrowed his eyes.

As the wheel slowed down, all those eyes saw the same thing; a dark little hole in the canvas, not eight inches from Frank's right elbow.

Samuel Kingston raised both arms to a massive cheer. "Spin him again, boys!" he shouted.

This time he fired twice before the wheel slowed. One bullet near Frank's right ear, another between his legs. Balum blinked harder. His eyes had been fixed on Kingston, and what he saw was a mess. A strange stance, a clumsy aim. Kingston's whole body jerked each time he fired as if he was completely unaccustomed to the recoil of a gun.

But the holes were real enough.

The crowd was shrieking and clapping and by the torchlight Balum searched their faces. He found the sheriff, the deputies. He found Bucky and Andy Fletcher and the other two that rode with them. Rhett Hastings was there. The kid from the poker game. The liveryboy. He recognized several men who had been manning the booths, but he couldn't find Barney Harrington.

He was still searching for Barney when Kingston fired his fourth shot. The other elbow. The hole about eight inches away. Frank's expression showed no fear. No concern. Balum wondered how many times he had done this. How many times could a man cheat death?

The final shot missed Frank's left ear by the same distance as the others, and before Kingston launched into his final speech, Balum started for the cabin.

27

He took the long way back with Betty and Sue Ellen chattering beside him like a couple of clucking hens. They oohed and ahhed at Kingston's marksmanship and at his fine speech. They remarked on Frank's bravery.

Balum offered no comment. One half of his mind was convinced the show was crooked, while the other half was opening the door to self-doubt. He replayed the shoutout with Andy Fletcher sixty times over in his mind before they reached the cabin door.

"Balum, honey, what's the matter?"

He looked up as if coming out of a dreamstate. Sue Ellen put her hand on his elbow.

"Nothing," he said. "I'm fine."

"You just need some rest, that's all. Isn't that right, Betty?"

"That's right." She lit the candle and set it over the table. "He just needs some rest."

In the soft glow of candlelight the women removed their jackets. They slipped off their boots. They made a show of bashfulness while they unbuttoned their blouses; bats of their eyelids, a turn of their shoulders. They giggled and pretended to shoo him away. He didn't move. He watched.

If it was Island Syndrome or simple lunacy, he didn't care. In under three days the women had transformed from worn-out old crones to supple-skinned goddesses. Their lips were full and their skin radiant, curves everywhere, long flowing hair. The smell of perfume mingled with the scent of their skin. The scent of their cunts.

"Balum, shame on you," Sue Ellen teased. She cupped her breasts in one arm and hugged them tight against her.

"You aren't going to sleep with all those clothes on, are you, Balum?" said Betty.

He kicked his boots off and unbuckled his gunbelt. "No, ma'am."

The women peeked over their shoulders at him while they shimmied into their nighties. When he slid his trousers down and stepped out of them their faces froze.

His cock was nearly ripping through his underwear. It pushed against the fabric like a whaler's harpoon, a spear aimed at its quarry. He tucked his thumbs beneath the waistband and pulled them off.

"Balum," Sue Ellen said softly.

Naked he stood before them. He'd not shaved in a week, and a bath was long overdue. The scar on his chest was black and angry, and silhouetted in that orange light he appeared more beast than man, a heavily-muscled brute with wide shoulders, meaty thighs, and a craving for carnal acts.

In three steps he reached Sue Ellen. He slid one hand up the back of her neck and grabbed a fistful of hair and guided her onto her knees. She didn't resist. She opened her mouth and took the length of him down her throat, and when he pulled her hair back she only looked up at him with eyes wide-open and moaned softly as she sucked.

Betty clapped a hand over her mouth. Her eyes were fixed on Sue Ellen. Balum raised a hand and called her closer. She obeyed. She crossed the room like a woman in a trance, closed her eyes when Balum took her gently by the chin, and when he slid his tongue into her mouth she moaned and clung to him as if her knees might give way beneath her.

He released her chin and ran his hand down her throat, over her breasts, down her belly to her cunt. He sank his fingers into the wet crease of her pussy, all the while guiding Sue Ellen's mouth along his shaft. He hadn't let her hair go; his grip had only tightened. He pulled her head back. Her lips were parted, her breath coming hard. Her eyes rolled onto Betty's cunt, and when Balum pulled his fingers dripping from it and brought them to Sue Ellen's mouth, she took them eagerly, sucking and moaning and fingering herself beneath her nightie.

"Balum," Betty moaned in his ear, "I want to feel you inside of me." She turned to her bed and crawled onto it with her ass barely covered beneath the hem of the nightie. She flipped it up. She turned her head and caught his eye and gave her ass a wiggle.

Balum let go of Sue Ellen's hair. In two strides he reached the edge of the bed. He grabbed Betty by the hips and sank his cock into her with a thrust that caused her to collapse onto her forearms. She screamed, and her screams were muffled into the mattress and muffled by the brutal strikes of his hips against her ass.

Sue Ellen crawled over on hands and knees and when Balum saw her there beside him with her mouth wet and open, he grabbed her again by the hair and pulled his throbbing dick from Betty's cunt. It stood in the cold cabin air only a moment, then Sue Ellen grabbed it and swallowed it whole, gagging and drooling and making noises unfit for even a brothel whore.

Betty regained her elbows and turned around on the bed. Her face hung over the side. She was almost cheek to cheek with Sue Ellen.

"I want to taste it," she said. Her voice was like a schoolgirl's, pleading, begging. Balum drew it from Sue Ellen's lips and plunged it into Betty's mouth, and when her eyes bulged at the size of it filling her throat, he could hold out no longer, and he came, a great burst of cum exploding down her throat, his legs quaking. He grabbed her head in both hands and gave her another heavy thrust, and when he pulled it out, Sue Ellen snatched his cock by the base to slurp the last bits of cum glistening from its head.

A minute later he fell into Sue Ellen's bed more exhausted than after a day's work in the lumbercamps. He was asleep before she'd crawled in bed with him.

He woke to the candle still burning. It had burned by half. A mound of wax had dripped and hardened all around it. He should have been asleep, bone-weary and dog-tired, but he was not. He was hard as a rock, and Sue Ellen lay naked beside him. He leaned over and took a nipple in his mouth. She moaned. She ran her sleepy fingers through his hair. When he crawled onto her she woke fully, and when he plunged his cock inside her she let out a wail that would have woken half the neighborhood if he had not clamped his hand over her mouth. He drilled her like an animal, his hand tight over mouth, the two of them with their eyes locked together.

Three hours later he woke again and this time the candle was no more than a nub in its saucer. He rose. Went to Betty's bedside.

He fucked her ragged and in the morning they were at it again, all three of them; Betty and Sue Ellen bent over the table, Balum switching back and forth from one to the other. The cabin was an echochamber of moans and sultry panting, the air pungent with the smell of sex, and it was into this den of debauchery that Meredith opened the door.

She held a handbag in one hand. She dropped it. The whites of her eyes were enormous above her open jaw, which she slapped a hand to as if to stifle a scream.

Balum pulled himself from Betty's snatch and went to the door with his cock bearing down on Meredith like a bayonet. He grabbed her by the arm and pulled her inside and slammed the door behind her.

"Balum!" she yelped.

She wore a petticoat over a burgundy skirt. A bonnet with a lace veil over her head. Lace ruffles adorned the ends of her sleeves, a lace bow encircled her neckline. Balum had all these things off and cast aside before she fully seemed to comprehend what was taking place.

She tried to argue, but her eyes kept dropping to his swollen cock, still wet with Betty's juices.

"Balum," was all she said, almost breathless. Her blouse

went sailing across the room.

Sue Ellen and Betty grinned delightedly. Their faces were drenched in sweat. Strings of wet hair were matted to their brows.

"See if you can quench him, Meredith," giggled Sue Ellen. "He's completely worn us out."

Meredith slapped Balum's hand from her belly. "Balum, stop it. What's gotten into you?" She slapped him again. Not hard. A gentle tap.

He spun her around and bent her over the table between Betty and Sue Ellen.

"Balum!" she squealed again, but there was no resistance in her. She even drew her knees together to allow her skirt to fall, and after he'd flung it aside she parted them again. She arched her bottom in the air.

Still, she feigned protest. "Balum, how dare you," she scolded while she parted her thighs further.

The sight of her wet pussy before him sent his heart into his throat. Her bottom was firm and perfectly round, her waist petite. She offered another preposterous attempt at admonishment, and he stopped with the head of his dick resting against her hot cunt.

"No?" he said.

She was sprawled over the tabletop with her neck twisted around and her eyes watching him. Both hands gripped the far table ledge.

"Okay," he said, and started to pull away.

She let the table go with one hand and swung her arm around behind her. She found his cock there waiting. She grabbed it firmly by the base and guided it back, caressing the head along the edge of her pussy, then shoved him in.

She lay her cheek against the table and closed her eyes. Her legs quivered. She gripped the table ledge again and whimpered while he drove himself into her. He rode her in long smooth strides, gradually building to harder, violent strokes, taking pleasure in the soft little grunts she let out in perfect rhythm.

Betty and Sue Ellen came to either side of him and kissed his neck, his shoulders. They ran their hands along his back and over the scar on his chest. Sue Ellen spread Meredith's ass cheeks open and commented on how wet she was, how sensual she found the sight of his dick sliding in and out of Meredith's young pussy.

He held her by the waist, pounding her, and when she came, she came with a wail that sent a hot gusher of cum exploding into her cunt. He held her to him, the last throbs of ejaculation spewing inside her, until her wails died to a whimper.

She pushed herself up from the table and turned around. Cum ran down her thighs.

"Balum," she said. She was half-laughing. She ran her fingers up the inside of her leg and shook her head. "Shame on you."

"You got what you came for."

"Oh, you think I came for this?"

"Well didn't you?"

"I'll admit it was a delightful little surprise, but no. I didn't come to be ravaged by a horny beast."

"What did you come for then?"

She leaned forward and took his cock in her hand. It was still thick. It grew as she stroked it. "I came to tell you that your gun is ready. Not this one," she squeezed his cock. "The other one. The Dragoon."

28

To keep him from crossing town in broad daylight all three women had to stand in the doorway as living barricades. They tried reasoning with him, pleading, begging, threatening. Eight hours remained until nightfall, and what finally convinced him were promises of sexual deviancy beyond what Balum could resist.

When he did finally slip into the street it was hours later in the black of night, on weak legs and aching loins, but with a mind as clear as springwater.

The carnival had packed up and moved out early that morning. The poker tournament was over. The streets were nearly bare. Still, Balum moved cautiously. At the corner of Main Street he crouched and studied the horses at the hitch rails, the buggies, the coal vendor pushing a wheelbarrow up the center of the street and hawking his product in a voice that rang hollow through the town. Balum stuck a wad of chaw in his lip and waited for him to pass.

When he reached Tom Brown's, he didn't even need to knock. The gunsmith had been keeping watch through the window.

"I figured you'd come," Tom Brown pulled him inside.

He narrowed an eye when he saw Balum in the full light of the workshop. "You look like you've been through eighteen rounds with an Indian wrestler. What happened to you?"

"Island Syndrome," said Balum.

Tom Brown bent laughing at the waist, hands on his knees, his head shaking. "You old dog," he said. "Come over here and look at what I got for you. You're gonna be tickled."

The weapon rested over a shop rag, polished so its bluish-black gunmetal shone with a perfect glint. Balum picked it up. The way the Colt .45 cylinder fit into the body of the Dragoon was a beautiful thing to see, a beautiful thing to feel. The weight of the gun balanced itself of its own accord in his hand. A perfect fit.

"I expect you'll want to see how she fires," said Tom Brown.

"I do."

"Let's take a little walk then. Grab them shells and come with me."

They crossed the empty carnival grounds and continued on through a field of sagebrush until they were nearly a half-mile outside town. While they walked, Tom Brown brought up the Kingston Crackshot.

"I saw it," said Balum.

"Did you? What did you think?"

"I've been going over that since last night," said Balum. "Fact is, I don't know what to make of it. Kingston didn't look comfortable handling that gun, but he did what he said he would; he put those bullets right where he wanted."

"That he did."

"I'll tell you what, I wouldn't allow myself to get tied to that wheel. Not with him handling that gun like it was the first time in his life."

"But like you said," the gunsmith looked back at him. "His shots were true."

"They were last night, anyway. How many times can he get lucky though?"

"You think it was luck?"

"Hell, I don't know."

They came to a stop. Tom Brown bent over, hunting for his target cans. He rummaged one out of the grass and walked off with it. "Here's the problem," he said as he walked. "That assistant of his doesn't seem to mind getting strapped up there."

"He's either confident or a fool," said Balum.

"Or there's something else."

"You figure it out, you tell me."

Tom Brown set the can on a rock and came swishing back through the sagebrush. "You don't know how giddy I am to see this," he said. "Your name isn't one that's known to everyone, and I expect you'd like to keep it that way. But to a man in my profession, word gets around. I've heard you're maybe the fastest, most accurate shot a man will ever see."

"I guess you didn't hear about yesterday then."

"I heard what happened," said the gunsmith. "It doesn't change my opinion. You were raised on that Dragoon. It's become almost a part of your body. Then all of the sudden that part of your body changes; it has a different length, a different weight, a different feel. No," he shook his head.

"This right here," he pointed a finger at the can twinkling in the moonlight, "is going to prove that."

Balum took the Colt Army revolver out of his holster and slid it into the back of his waistband. He dropped the Dragoon in its place.

Already it felt right. That familiar weight on his hip. He drew.

He didn't draw quickly, at least not in his own estimation; he drew smoothly, cleanly, a motion that brought with it a fair degree of pleasure. Everything about it was right. His thumb dragged the hammer back and his finger caught the familiar steel of the trigger and he fired. When the echo of the shot died away, Tom Brown rubbed his eyes. He took a step forward. He looked at Balum.

He had missed again.

"Give me that." The gunsmith grabbed the weapon and gave it a cursory look and handed it back. "Try it again."

Balum fired. He fired all remaining chambers and the can never moved.

The two men stood in silence a moment. Two solemn figures in the blue light of the moon. A low breeze through the sage.

"Wait a minute," said Tom Brown, "What cartridges did you grab?"

"The ones you told me to. The ones sitting on the workbench."

"Let me see."

Balum pulled one from his pocket and handed it over. The gunsmith held it up to the moon and twisted it and let out a laugh.

"You're shooting blanks!"

"Blanks?"

"There's no bullets in them. They got the powder, the wad, the plug, but no bullet. They just go bang, is all."

"Well what the hell do you have them laying around for?"

"Farmers, mostly. They've got bird problems around here. Some say they can lose thirty percent of their crop to birds. Trying to shoot them is a waste of time, but they scare easy enough. The farmers buy the blanks and send their kids into the fields. The kids have fun, and it's safer that way."

Balum breathed easier. He even laughed. "I thought I was losing my mind for a minute."

"Here," Tom Brown stuck a hand in his coat pocket. "Try these."

Four cartridges were all he had. Balum loaded them. He looked at the gunsmith and he looked at the can, then he fired. The can went skipping into the sagebrush. Before it stopped, Balum shot again. The can whined and bounced, and the next bullet kicked it three feet into the air. Mid-flight, Balum shot it through the center.

Tom Brown let out a whoop. "That's what I wanted to see!"

"You'll see a lot more tomorrow," said Balum. "Just don't send me off with the wrong cartridges."

29

He shared Betty's bed that night. He did not disturb her when he woke, nor Sue Ellen, asleep on the other side of the room. He sat at the table and tucked a wad of tobacco in his lip and thought about the four men in town that would face him in the street that day.

He felt no remorse. They had no reason to quit; they would be confident after having seen him bungle the Colt Army. Before the day was over they would be dead.

He left the cabin before the noonday sun had struck, his belly empty and the Dragoon fully loaded. He wore his hat eased back on his head. He tucked the Colt Army in back of his waistband, just in case. Sue Ellen and Betty had promised to stay put, but when he reached the end of the lane he caught them following. He made no effort to send them away.

With four men combing the city streets it would be a long day of cat and mouse. A dangerous day. Killing one would make the other three more wary. Once he killed two, that would leave two others nervous enough not to face him head-on, but instead shoot him in the back. Big Tom's men were not beyond that.

And so he did the most logical thing. Or the most foolish.

He walked down the center of Main Street and stopped a stone's throw from Claire's Creamery and called them out.

The first heads to appear were the locals. The leatherworker, the liveryboy, cooks from the restaurants. The sheriff came out of the barbershop with his face lathered in white cream, his freshly-shaven deputies right behind. Meredith was there. Tom Brown, too.

When Big Tom's men sauntered into the street they did so together as if they had talked it over in an alleyway and agreed to gun him down together. A smart choice for a pack of cowards. Their footfalls in the dust carried across town. The jangle of their spurs, the rustle of clothing. They stopped at fifty paces and spread out. The sounds of their movements vanished with them.

"Andy, Bucky, you other two," said Balum. "I'm going to speak real clear so there's no misunderstanding. You've come to kill and rob me, and I've little doubt you aim to ride up the trail and murder my friends. None of that is going to happen. So listen here; there's two ways out of it. One, you can turn yourself in to the sheriff over there," Balum raised his left arm toward the barbershop where the sheriff was wiping a towel across his face. "Or two, you can try your luck with those guns you're wearing. So make up your minds. Either way, this ends here."

Whatever conversation there was, Balum couldn't hear it. Their lips moved, but their eyes stayed firm. Then their lips stilled. All four stood with their hands inches from their guns.

By some unseen accord, they drew. Who drew first was hard to tell, all four slapped iron together, and then the

Dragoon was in Balum's hand and blasting like a cannon down the length of Main Street.

He put his first bullet through Andy Fletcher's sternum, just at the base of his throat. It tore through the soft flesh and took half the vertebrae of his neck away upon its exit. The two unknowns he shot through the heart and lungs. Bucky the drunkard came last. He had never shown any sign of a steady hand, no inclination for speed, but he was faster than Balum expected. His gun whipped almost as quickly as Andy's had, but his itchy finger pulled back on the trigger too quickly and the bullet burrowed into the dust at Balum's feet. He never got another shot. A .45 bullet caught him in the right eye and spun him around, and Balum's next bullet tore the top of his skull away. Bucky flopped to the ground in a tangle of arms and legs. Blood gushed into the dust and pooled in a dark murky puddle around him.

It seemed to take a long time for the reports of gunfire to fade. They echoed through the alleyways and over the rooftops, and the townsfolk stood gawking under the reverberations until the street returned to silence.

First to move was the sheriff. He threw the barber's towel to the ground and aimed a finger at Balum. "You listen here…"

"Shut your mouth," Balum's voice boomed as loud as the Dragoon. He finished thumbing cartridges into the cylinder and swatted it closed and let the gun hang alongside his thigh. "All up and down the prairie are two-bit sheriffs just like yourself. They sit at their desks with their feet up and take the townsfolk's money, and when trouble comes into town they scurry away like rodents to their holes, making excuses that don't square and don't matter. You've got no shame. You just let a gang of thieves come through here and rob these good people of their money. You let yourself be bought off by what, a riding crop for your wife? You let these four deadbeats walk around free," he swung the Dragoon over the four deadmen. "And so now I've gone and done your work for you. Well, Sheriff, I'm done working. You can bury them. And you all," he looked over the crowd. "I'd suggest you all find yourself a new sheriff once he's raised the tombstones."

He holstered the weapon. He turned his back on the sheriff and the deputies and everyone else; Meredith, Sue Ellen and Betty, Tom Brown, then he walked back past Claire's Creamery and out to the edge of town where the livery sat nearly empty.

He had just reached it when the liveryboy came running up behind.

"You ain't gone and sold my roan now, have you, son?" said Balum. "I only paid for a single night."

"No, sir, I've kept him fed and watered. He needed a good combing down and I done that too."

At the sound of Balum's voice, the roan poked its head over the stall gate. Balum scratched its jaw, patted its neck. He threw the blanket over its back, then the saddle, then the bridle and reins.

"I appreciate what you've done," said Balum. "The thing is, I've gone and wasted all my money. I've got nothing to pay you with."

"That's alright, mister. Seeing what you did back there was

worth it."

Balum looked at the boy. A hard-working lad. Honest. He reached around to the small of his back and pulled the Colt Army revolver from his waistband and held it out.

"Here," he said.

"You mean to give me that?"

"You've earned it. Maybe once you've learned to use it you can take the badge off that no-good sheriff's vest and put it on your own. This town needs an honest hand to run it." He led the roan down the line of stalls and into the sun. The boy followed.

"Why don't you stay, mister? You could be sheriff. Them dancehall ladies sure would like it," he grinned.

Balum swung into the saddle. "Those carnival crooks need dealing with. Besides, I've got my own woman waiting for me up the trail, and there ain't another from here to Albany that can hold a candle to her."

He tipped his hat at the boy and turned the roan out of town. "So long, son," he said, and was gone.

30

At some point during the four-day ride to Fairview, Balum figured he'd shoot himself a nice fat hare, a pheasant, maybe an antelope if he was lucky. He rode with his Winchester laid across his saddle, eyes alert, ready.

Instead all he found were the discarded scraps of chuckwagon grub tossed alongside the rut tracks of Samuel Kingston's traveling carnival show. He found empty bean cans burnt and blackened within the ashes of their campfires. An empty flour sack. Coffee dregs.

The roan got its fill on grass, but Balum rode with an empty belly that had started to gnaw at his ribcage by the time he drew within sight of Fairview. It wasn't the town he saw; night had fallen, and the impoverished citizenry owned few lanterns by which to light it. Instead he saw a hundred torches burning on the plain. A throng of glowing faces. Kingston on his wooden platform.

Balum nudged the roan to a trot. He realized he was grinding his teeth, but he couldn't relax. His neck throbbed. The urge to feel bones crunching beneath his fist was overwhelming. He'd come through Fairview before; a poorly named town full of destitutes. They had hardly any money for candles, a kerosine lantern was a luxury, and here they were spending what few pennies they had on a con man's show.

The wheel was already spinning when Balum pulled the roan to a stop at the far back of the crowd. From atop the saddle he saw the same thing he'd seen in Cumberland; a sloppy draw, an awkward aim, five bullets tearing holes through the canvas. They landed eight inches from Frank's face and limbs, same as before.

The crowd ate it up. Before they had fully dispersed, Kingston's men were already dismantling the show. They broke down the platform, loaded the fortress of hay onto the wagons bale by bale and, in the dark of night, shoved northward as if to be rid of Fairview and its beggarly populace forever.

Balum remained. He needed food. Water. He drifted into town but there was not an open establishment to be found, and eventually he led the roan away and made a cold camp on the plain.

In the morning he made his way to the Fairview Tavern where he was turned away by a sallow proprietor. "I don't run no tabs, and I don't do handouts. If you're that hard up for a plate of food, mister, I suggest you earn it by the sweat of your back."

"Show me where," said Balum.

"Have you ever butchered hogs?"

An hour later Balum was a quarter-mile outside town, knee deep in blood. A two-hundred pound hog lay split open before him. The man on the other side was holding the hog's ribs apart, allowing room for Balum to reach his arm into the cavity and pull out the heart and lungs and drop it into the metal bucket the man's wife held at the ready.

It was the first of eight pigs they butchered that day. By the end of it Balum reeked of blood and spilled intestines, and his boots were forever stained a dark burgundy red.

For his work he was fed at the man's table that night. Pork liver and chops. The man's wife had a haggard look about her and kept her eyes on her plate, the four children as well, but the pig farmer himself was pleased with the day's work, and suddenly eager to chat. Invariably the conversations turned to the Kingston Crackshot.

"I don't blame them for not setting up the whole carnival show," he said through a mouthful of liver. "But we sure was lucky to see that shooting. I ain't never seen nothing like it in all my life. It was worth every penny we paid."

"Why don't you think he set it up?"

"The carnival? Wouldn't have been worth his time. I don't reckon he'll set the whole show up again until he reaches Denver."

"That's where the people are," agreed Balum.

"Aye. And the poker. Ain't you heard? Two-thousand dollars in prize money. That's more money than I've ever seen in my life." The pig farm sucked the juices from his fingers and reached across the table for the grits. "A man wins that kind of money and he don't got to butcher no more swine as long as he lives! Does he, honey?"

His wife only shook her head and worked a mouthful of grizzle around her teeth.

On the farmer's insistence Balum spent the night on their

cabin floor. He did not sleep well; the farmer's wife snored, and the children were up and fighting before the sun rose. He did accept a slab of bacon and a pork chop wrapped in newspaper before he rode out, and when he finally left sight of Fairview, it was on a full belly and a worried mind.

That poker tournament would call in gamblers from far and wide, and right in the middle of it would be Chester. He was more than just a good gambler; he was one of the best. But he worked on skill, not trickery. Against Rhett Hastings and his cronies he would see his money disappear like a moth into the flames.

The thought of it stayed with him all that day. It was there when he made his fire at night, there while he cooked his pork chop, and when he woke in the morning it had fermented into a great brooding thing that hung over him five more days on the trail until the sound of cattle lowing in the valleys finally snapped him from his worries.

Cattle by the hundreds. They roamed in small groups, some laying out in the noonday sun, their hides like great brown blotches peppering the endless grass. It meant Crenshaw was near.

Despite the smell of stew meat drifting from the inns, it was not his empty belly that occupied Balum's mind when he rode into town, but the sight of telegraph poles stretching down the valley in a thin jagged line. He followed them to where they disappeared into a tarpaper roof. His eyes dropped to the doorway. Above it a sign read TELEGRAPH OFFICE.

The fellow inside only shrugged his shoulders and offered a sympathetic look. "I'm sorry, mister, but the going rate is twenty cents a word, and someone's got to pay it."

"I'll work it off."

"Doing what?"

"Whatever there is to do. Just name it."

The telegraph operator scratched his nose while he thought on it. "I wish there was something, I truly do. But the fact is, folks is hard up around here. I'm sorry."

He tried the sheriff next. He was the only lawman from Denver to San Antonio that was worth his salt, aside from Ross Buckling. Balum found him at his desk, mired in a stack of papers.

"Afternoon, Sheriff."

The sheriff picked his head out of the papers. He was big around in the torso and wore a thick silver mustache that could use a combing.

He eyed Balum head to toe. "I know you, don't I?"

"I came through a few months back escorting a prisoner to San Antonio. He stayed the night in one of your jail cells here."

The sheriff slapped his desk. "That's right. I remember. You and that Indian friend of yours. A black man too, if I remember right."

"Speaking of them, did Joe pass this way? The Apache? He would have had a Mexican woman with him."

"Over a week ago they did."

"Everything alright?"

"They didn't stir up no trouble, if that's what you mean. Not like that damn pack of thieves that come through here last night."

"Are you talking about the carnival show?"

"I am. They wanted to set up some tinhorn sharpshooting nonsense. I can smell a crook a mile out, and these had the stink all over them, so I shut it down. Told 'em to scram. Only they didn't. They came into town and into the bars and taverns, and they worked my people over for a sightload of money." The sheriff wiped a hand down his mustache. "You never seen such tricksters as these. All sorts of swindles they had, and this morning I wake up to find them long gone and a line of angry townsfolk at my door."

"They aren't the first," said Balum. "Kingston and his men have been working folks over from here to Texas. They're on their way to the poker tournament in Denver now. That's why I'm here; I need to ask a favor."

"Let's hear it."

"I need to send a telegram up that way."

"It's already done. I sent one up the road to Muckville, another to Denver, another clear to Cheyenne. Told 'em to get ready for a pack of crooks."

"Well that's good." Balum took his hat off and ran a hand through his hair. "Only the telegram I want to send is personal. See, there's a group of cardsharps that tag along with Kingston, and I'd like to warn a friend of mine in Denver."

"I expect you do."

"The thing is, I'm flat broke."

The sheriff smoothed his mustache again. "I see what you're driving at," he said. "But look what I got here," he tapped the stacks of papers.

"I see them."

"Complaints, every last one of them. I got folks here that lost money in card bets, bar bets, games with match sticks, and one fellow who paid thirty dollars for a pocket watch that ain't worth a Confederate penny. All in the space of a night. They all want their money back, and they ain't gonna get it. It's gone." He snorted, which riffled the hairs of his mustache. "I'd give them something out of the City Commission, but the pittance that was there just got spent on those telegrams I sent. So there you have it. The coffers have done been raided, the cabinets are bare. I'm sorry."

Balum put his hat back on. He turned to the door.

"I can at least get you a hot meal before you go," the sheriff said behind him. "You look like you could use it."

The meal consisted of tough meat in a weak broth, and before the sun went down that night, Balum's stomach was already back to rumbling.

He made camp a couple miles north of town. A fire to warm him. An endless sweep of starlit skies to gaze upon. He staked the roan on a patch of good grass and crawled beneath his blanket and found Cassiopeia, Orion, the two dippers hanging in the void. The fire burned itself to coals. He'd just drifted to sleep when the roan snorted.

Balum opened his eyes. The horse turned and stomped a hoof, and Balum grabbed the Dragoon from beside his head and shot out of his blankets and into the grass.

<h1 style="text-align:center">31</h1>

After a minute of silence, the roan went back to grazing. Balum lowered his gun. It was probably his damn belly gurgling like a pot of boiling tar that had gotten the horse's ears up. Still, he waited. He could wait a long time in the dark, he'd done it plenty of times before. The first to move was usually the first to catch a bullet.

He didn't have to wait long. The starlight was good enough to pick out shapes on the grass, silhouettes, movement, and the exact shape his eyes caught was a figure no more than five feet tall and wearing a dress. A child.

She walked a few steps closer. "Mister Balum?"

Balum let the hammer down. He scanned the open prairie and found nothing there that shouldn't be there. Nothing but the girl.

She came right up to the edge of the coals. "I'm looking for Mister Balum."

"Well you found me," Balum said from the grass. "What do you want?"

"I need your help. I mean, my momma needs your help."

He rose out of his crouch and walked to the dying campfire where he could see her better.

"How old are you?"

"I'm twelve."

"You shouldn't be out in the dark like this. What's this about your momma? Does she know you're out here?"

"No."

"Well get on back home then."

"Not until you hear me out."

Only a few red embers glowed beneath the ashes. A few sticks of kindling remained, and after Balum had eased them into the heart of the coals and coaxed the fire back to life, he motioned for her to sit, and together they warmed their hands as she told her story.

She was sparse with her words. The story she told needed no exaggeration.

Several months back, her father, grandfather, grandmother, and brother, were shot and killed by a gang of outlaws. All for hardly one-hundred dollars cash. Her mother was left to run the ranch, the Circle J Bar, which was a task far beyond the abilities of any one person. The ranch was falling to ruin, the cattle scattered, and her mother's scant savings gone.

"It's a foul thing, and I'm sorry for you," said Balum. "But here's some consolation you can take back to your mother. Those boys that killed your family, those were the Bell Brothers. Every last one of them is dead. I know that for a fact because I had a hand in the killing. Now about your ranch, I can't do nothing about that. I got no time to round up cattle or keep up with repairs. I need to get on up the trail. I'm sorry."

"I didn't ask you to round up cattle or keep up with repairs."

"Well what are you asking then?"

"I'm asking you to run off the no-good malingerer that my momma hired to do all those things. He took her money but he ain't done nothing except to spread lies and rumors about us. He's squatting in my grandpa's house and he won't leave, and my momma don't know what to do. She don't do nothing but cry no more."

"So what do you want me to do about it?"

"Run him off. My momma said you were the man to do it."

"Did she?"

"She heard from the sheriff you were in town. He said you were a lawman once, and that you ain't no more, but if ever there was a man that walked both sides of the law and got away with it, it was you."

"He said all that?"

"He did," said the girl.

"What's this fellow's name? The squatter."

"Gary Cashews."

Balum's face wrinkled. "That sounds made up."

"My momma thinks the same thing."

"Why doesn't the sheriff run him off?"

"It's out of his jurisdiction, is what he says. My grandpa's cabin is over the county line, and the sheriff there don't get along with ours. They been feuding for years. He's letting Gary stay there just to stick it in the sheriff's craw."

Balum shoved another stick into the fire.

The girl stood up. "Well are you coming or ain't you?"

"Shoot," said Balum. He prodded the fire. The fact was, he didn't have time for this. He needed to be riding by first light. He had a long way to go, and he wouldn't make it by stopping to kick out every deadbeat squatter he ran into along the way. He said as much.

"Well you won't make it half-starved, neither," said the girl.

Balum stopped poking at the fire. He set his eyes on the girl.

She was laughing. "I can hear your belly growling like it's gonna jump up and go somewhere's else. My momma ain't got no money, but at least she'll feed you."

His belly jerked at the prospect of food.

"How far is it?"

"Five, six miles."

"Kick that fire out. I'll saddle the roan."

She rode behind him with her arms clutched at his waist and her mouth going a mile a minute. Her name was Eva. She liked riding, liked flowers, liked a boy named Tommy. She wondered if Balum was going to have to shoot Gary Cashews. If he was, she wanted to see it.

Balum gave no answer. He'd let himself get roped into a squatter's feud on nothing more than the promise of a meal, and he cursed himself for it. Such goes a man's fortune when he's fool enough to let himself be outwitted, outmaneuvered, swindled, snookered and conned. It was his own fault he was half starved and penniless. He hadn't planned on butchering hogs, and he sure as hell never thought he would be riding off-course to play knight to a helpless widow. Yet here he was. Listening to a twelve year old girl prattle on about some boy she liked.

She was still chattering when they rode past a cow barn and an untended pole corral. Even in the dim starlight it was obvious that nearly every aspect of the homestead needed work. A light shone through the cabin window. A kerosine lantern.

The door swung open and a woman holding an old Ferguson rifle appeared in it.

Eva's arms tightened on Balum's waist. "Momma, don't shoot!"

"Eva?"

"I got Mister Balum with me. He's gonna get rid of that good-for-nothing Gary, you'll see."

Her name was Ruth, and by the look of her face and hands she was taking on the work of six men. While she warmed a pot of stew she told him the story. It was the same as Eva had told him, only more detailed.

This Gary Cashews had drifted in out of nowhere, and when he sussed out Ruth's situation he had talked himself up. He had promised her hard work in exchange for her father's cabin, and what she got in return was a bum. And not only a bum, but a spreader of lies. They started soon after she refused his advances. He called her a whore, a lush. He spread rumors that she beat her child, practiced witchery, that she ran naked in the fields and copulated with animals.

She cried as she told him this, and her tears fell into the pot.

"Where is he now?" said Balum.

"In the cabin, I expect."

"Is he armed?"

Ruth nodded. She wiped a tear from her cheek while she ladled hot stew into three bowls.

"And all you want is for him to be out of the cabin?" said Balum.

"I want him gone. Away from here."

"What about his things? His belongings?"

"He doesn't have any. None to speak of anyway. When he arrived he didn't even have a horse to his name, so I loaned him an old mare." Her mouth tightened. "He can keep it, as long as he rides away on it and never comes back. I just want him out of my life."

The stew was hot and the flavor deep from sitting three days in the pot, but with the widow wiping tears from her cheeks and Eva watching her mother helpless and beat, it didn't go down so well. He gulped down the last spoonful and put his hat back on.

"I know it's late," he said, "but if you want him out, now's the time to do it. Are you up for a ride?"

They left Eva alone and rode out of the homestead in a gallop, Balum on his roan, and Ruth on a stocky-legged filly that had the single-minded mentality of a racehorse. When they reached the cabin they slowed to a walk and finally stopped completely to observe from a distance.

Trash littered the yard. Feral cats slunk in the uncut grass. There were no dogs to announce their arrival, no sound or lights or signs of life within the cabin, but the old mare was there, slack-ribbed and shrunken. A spent horse, too long uncared for.

Balum swung off the saddle. He passed the reins to Ruth and motioned for her to stay put, then made his way through the trash to the cabin door. He set his hand on the butt of the Dragoon. He tried the handle. Locked.

For a moment he considered his options. First the polite ones; the ones a sheriff or a deputy would employ. Problem was, they took too long. The knocking, the talking, the arguing and cajoling. And Balum didn't have the time. From what Ruth had told him, Gary was cut from the same cloth as Shane Carly. A deadbeat through and through.

He went back up through the grass to where Ruth waited.

"What's wrong?"

"Ma'am, if you don't mind a little damage to your cabin…"

"Burn him out for all I care."

"Alright then."

He slid the Winchester from the scabbard and went back the way he'd come. Two feet from the door he stopped. He set the end of the barrel against the lock and turned his head and fired.

Shards of wood stung him in the face. The door creaked open. He kicked it clean through and stepped into a room filled with refuse, old newspapers, scraps of tin. Cats everywhere. The smell of urine. Stale tobacco.

"Hey!"

Commotion from the side of the room.

Balum reached it under four paces and smashed the stock of the rifle into a figure rising from the bed. A wet crunch, a thud. He reached down and caught a greasy ponytail and dragged Gary through his piles of garbage and out the smashed door and into the yard.

By starlight he took sight of a man in his early fifties, long red hair, rumpled clothing. He was bleeding from the mouth. He moaned and set his fingers to his lips.

"Gary Cashews, you just got evicted. Get your ass on that old mare and ride out."

Gary took his fingers from his lips. They glistened wet with blood. He looked from them to Balum above him. "Who the hell are you?"

"Name is Balum."

"You got no right to kick me out. This is my house."

"It's not your house. And now you're leaving."

Gary shook his head. "I guess you ain't heard of squatter's rights. I'll have you know that according to the law—"

Balum slapped him. An open-handed wallop across the cheek. "This isn't your house, and I don't give a damn what the law says about squatter's rights. If you don't get up on that horse in the next minute, I'll pick you up and tie you over its back and let it take you wherever it's of a mind to. So get up."

"What about my things? My belongings? I got money in there."

"Ms. Ruth will be taking that as payment for the mare."

"You can't do this to me. It ain't legal. Why, I'm hardly

dressed!"

Balum grabbed him by his ponytail. Gary swatted his arms and screamed like a woman all the way to the mare.

"Get up on that horse and ride."

"Where am I supposed to go?"

"Anywhere that ain't here." Balum poked him with the barrel. "I'll give you two minutes to get her saddled. Otherwise you go bareback."

Gary stood with his hands at his sides. "You ain't gonna get away with this."

Balum poked him again. "It's over, Gary. Time to move on."

32

They found four dollars in an old tin can, half of which Ruth insisted he keep.

"I'd have done it just for the bowl of stew, ma'am," said Balum.

She pressed it into his hands. "I want you to have it. You have no idea how much this means to me."

He would rather have gone hungry than take the widow's money. But there was Chester to consider. An old friend, and one he owed many a debt to. And so he accepted.

The sun was up by the time they reached Ruth's cabin. Before he could say his goodbyes, Ruth woke Eva and told her to saddle an old gelding nearly sixteen hands tall. She had business in town to take care of, and she would appreciate an accompaniment to town.

On Eva's insistence Balum recounted the story of Gary's eviction not once, but twice. She howled with laughter just as hard the second time.

She was still giggling when they reached the edge of Crenshaw. It was the only sound to disturb the morning quiet. Before they were past the lumber yard a man hailed them from a corner. He wore a desperate look, his eyes whipping everywhere.

"Oh good sir, madame," he stuttered. "I mean not to disturb you, but I'm in an awful bind. You see, I've gone and lost my wife's ring, and I don't know what to do. You haven't seen it, by chance, have you?"

"No, I'm sorry," said Ruth.

"If you do, I'd gladly pay you for it. A fine reward; twenty dollars. It would be worth it just to get it back."

"I'm sorry, we've not seen it," said Ruth.

They rode on. Balum glanced once behind him. The man was already gone, back up through the lumber yard.

At the telegraph office he pulled up. "This is my stop, ma'am. I wish you well." He smiled at Eva. "You be good for your momma, you hear?"

He watched them ride up the street together. A woman and her daughter, two slight figures set against a world of hardship. Eva turned and waved. Balum waved back.

In the telegraph office he sent a message to Chester that said only, *Don't play poker with Rhett Hastings*. It cost him a dollar and twenty cents.

"Anything else?" asked the operator.

Balum looked at the coins remaining. Eighty cents. Enough to buy a pinch of flour, a tin of beans, maybe a slice of bacon. If he was prudent, it would keep him fed until Blacktown.

The hell with it.

"One more," he said. "This one to Cheyenne. Angelique is her name."

"And what'll it say?"

"I'm coming for you."

He stepped out of the telegraph office penniless again, but with a smile on his face and his heart warm at the thought of his woman. He unlooped the horse's reins from the hitch rail and threw a leg over the saddle. He had only put it to a trot when he caught Ruth and Eva engaged with a man outside the general store.

The man held a ring between his fingers. Whatever he was explaining, Balum couldn't hear it. He didn't need to. He put the roan to a gallop and came down on the swindler like a rodeo rider on a roping calf.

The man glanced up, but too late. The roan's shoulder caught him and sent him flying. He came off the ground still holding the ring. He raised his hands up in front of him and tried waving Balum off, but Balum had dropped from the saddle and was already on him. He caught the swindler with a right hook in the gut. The man doubled over. He dropped the ring. He sank to his knees and dry-heaved into the street.

"Balum!" Ruth jumped off her horse. "What on earth are you doing?"

"Saving you your money." He stepped back from the swindler who was coughing and spitting in the dirt. "It's a trick he must have picked up from the carnival folks. I reckon he told you he just happened to find that ring laying around. Offered to sell it to you. Cheap."

"He said he'd take two dollars for it."

"Ma'am," said Balum. "You'd have been out two dollars and stuck with a ring that ain't worth a damn." He prodded the man with his boot. "Get lost before I knock those teeth out."

The man staggered up and weaved a crooked path around the general store and out of sight.

Ruth put a hand on Balum's arm. "I could use a man like you around the ranch. There's so much to do. I promise there'll be more than just a bowl of stew if you come back with me."

He looked from Ruth to little Eva sitting on her great big gelding.

"I wish I could," he said. "But I'm needed up the road."

He gave her arm a squeeze. Let it go. He nodded once to Eva. Then he turned and caught the roan by the reins and swung into the saddle. He rode past the general store and past the sheriff's office, then he turned the roan's nose northward and set the beast to a gallop.

He looked back once, but the dust hung thick behind him. Ahead of him the air was clear. He took in a great big gulp of it and ignored the empty rumble roaring in the pit of his belly.

33

Still no game. No deer, no fish, no fowl. Not in all those miles of empty land and cold hard ground by which he made his pillow at night. He would have shot himself a prairie dog and eaten it over a fire of buffalo chips if he had to, but there was nothing but a trail of bent grass winding north to occupy his eyes. The passage of Kingston's troupe. Old campfires, flecks of hay.

He wondered why they needed so much hay. The wheel for the Kingston Crackshot was set up like a deep-seated drum laid over on its side. A dozen bales would do, yet they used five times that much.

He bit off a plug of tobacco and let his mind wrestle with it. He studied on it, let it go, came back around to it again. By the time he reached Muckville several days later, the matter had morphed into a conundrum that occupied every corner of his mind.

The sight of the town helped distract him. It was no different than he'd last seen it. It could take first prize in a filth contest if there were such a thing. The streets were made of hardened clay and not a single boardwalk had been built to keep the sludge from seeping beneath the storefront doors each time it rained. No one had seen fit to tear down the burned-out building beside the pig wallow. The only colors to the town were gray and brown. Not a flower or a blade of grass in sight.

Balum debated a long while whether to stop or ride on through. On his last visit he had drilled the sheriff in the mouth and locked him in his own cell for the night. He had also threatened the proprietor of the boarding house with a first-class whipping if he didn't serve Caleb and Joe. He hadn't made a single friend in town.

But Balum's belly won out, and he rode down the potted lane and dismounted at the general store. He explained his predicament to the store clerk, who only shrugged and waved him off. At the butchers he got the same. The dentist too. He tried the livery and the carpenter and found no helping hand or friendly smile, and finally he walked back to the boarding house and into the cramped eating hall where he nearly bumped into the sheriff slurping up a bowl of hominy.

The sheriff whipped his head up from his bowl. His nose was wrapped in muslin cloth and bent to one side. Old bruises discolored his cheekbones.

"Watch where you're…" He stopped and leaned back. He squinted. "I know you."

"Yes you do."

"You're that son of a bitch that came through here with a nigger and a half-breed and locked me in my cell."

The eating hall went quiet. Silverware lowered, eyes raised. The proprietor came out from the kitchen and stopped in the doorway with his arms loaded down with plates.

When Balum spoke, everyone listened. "It's that kind of talk that put you there. You can keep it up or you can try your hand at hospitality. That goes for all of you." He shot a look at the proprietor. "I've been on the road a long time. I've got no money and I've got a hole in my belly that needs filling. If anyone here has a job to do, I'll do it. Anything in exchange for a fair plate of grub."

One of the diners in back opened his mouth, but the sheriff shot a hand up.

"This is my town. I run it. What I say here is the law, and I say you take your begging ass up the road and don't come back."

"That's what you say?"

"You're goddamn right that's what I say!" The sheriff smacked a hand over the tabletop, sending the dishware clattering. "Do you see this?" He pointed at his nose. "Your half-breed friend did this. Came through here a week ago with a Mexican woman and thought he could sit down for a meal. Well I'll tell you something; here in Muckville we don't serve Mexicans and we don't serve savages." He crossed his arms. "And we don't serve bums. Now get out."

"Where are they now?"

"They ran off up the road like the cowards they are. If I ever see them around here again I'll put a bullet in them. Now get out."

Balum stood motionless. His stomach was doing flips over the smell of food, and in a spot in his head somewhere back between his eyes there was a small rage growing. He stepped to the sheriff's table and took hold of the bowl with his left hand. He slid it closer. He picked up the spoon. He raised a great big portion of hominy to his mouth and dumped it in. All the while his right hand remained an inch from the Dragoon at his hip.

The sheriff's eyes twitched. His jaw was clenched and his nostrils flared just beneath the wrapping of muslin cloth.

Balum smacked while he chewed. His eyes never left the sheriff. He swallowed and lowered the spoon back into the bowl.

"I've come a long way from San Antonio and I've seen a lot of deadbeat sheriffs, but you take top prize. Now I've made a fair offer to work in exchange for a meal, and you've decided to stop that. So I'm simply going to take it. I'm going to take that meal and you're not going to do a thing about it." He dipped the spoon back into the bowl and drew out another serving of hominy. He chewed and swallowed and aimed the spoon at the proprietor. "Take those plates of food and wrap them in newspaper. I'll be taking them with me."

The sheriff reached for his gun. He was seated only two feet from Balum, and Balum simply balled his right fist and drove his knuckles into the mound of muslin cloth at the center of the sheriff's face. The sheriff toppled backward. He hit the floor and rolled over clutching his freshly-broken nose, and Balum came up behind him and slid the lawman's gun from his holster.

"Wrap up those plates," he said again to the proprietor.

"What are you doing with our sheriff?"

Balum had him by the hair and was already halfway through the door. "I'm putting him away for a while. Maybe he'll learn some manners in jail. Now get that plate wrapped up or I'll put you in with him."

He rode out of town less than ten minutes later with two plates of food resting on the saddle horn and the keys to the jail cell jangling in his pocket. A mile outside town he took the keys out and flung them in the grass. A spell behind bars would set the sheriff's mind right. And if it didn't, Balum didn't give a damn. Either way, he didn't dwell on it. His mind was on Denver, on Angelique, on Chester and Samuel Kingston, on Rhett Hastings and the sweet taste of revenge that he wanted so dearly yet had not the slightest idea on how to attain.

Two days later he shot a jackrabbit at eighty yards while in the saddle. Not with the Winchester— it would have taken too long. He shot it with the Dragoon, and a clean shot it was, straight through the neck. It was the kind of shooting folks would roll their eyes at if they were to hear about it. A loping hare, the roan at a trot, and Balum at eighty yards. Yet there he sat at his fire that evening, the rabbit skinned and dressed and roasting on a spit over the flames.

There had been one witness to it. A red-haired ponytailed bum that Balum first spotted the day he rode out of Muckville. He noticed him again on his backtrail two days later. He found it mildly surprising that the beat-up mare could keep pace with the roan. But whatever Gary Cashews had in mind, Balum didn't care. The damn fool was more a nuisance than a threat.

Aside from the jackrabbit, he went hungry clear to Blacktown. Most any other white man riding into such a place unannounced would fare poorly. A beating at best, a bullet more likely. But this was a town of allies, and when folks saw who it was riding down the lane on the familiar roan, they poured into the streets with wide grins and hands eager to greet him.

The meal served at Caleb's table resembled more a royal banquet than an offering prepared by simple folk. He ate his share and half as much again. There was no need to tell the story of Joe and Valeria's battle with Big Tom; the two had passed through on their way north and the tales had all been told. Instead they begged him to recount his escape from the state penitentiary. A story they'd heard a hundred times over, and one of which they would never tire.

After he'd told it he asked about the carnival. "Their tracks lead up along the edge of town," he said.

"Shit, Balum," Caleb laughed. "Them fool crackers took one look at us and turned another shade of white. They gone up the road already."

"You're good to be rid of them," said Balum. "A pack of crooks is what they are." He told them about the Kingston Crackshot. He explained it in detail. How he couldn't figure it out.

"Ain't no way in hell I'm gonna stick my black ass on a wheel and let myself get shot at," said Caleb. "Some of them white folks are dumb, Balum, but ain't nobody that dumb. There's something crooked going on."

"I know it. I just can't find the angle."

"You want more chitlins? More greens?"

"All I want is a place to sleep." He threw a glance at Summer. She'd been flirting from the back of the cabin all night, and when he caught her eye she ran her tongue over her lips and smiled.

"You can lay your head anywhere you like," said Caleb. He waved a hand at the people crowding his house. "Go on now, you heard him. The man needs his shut eye."

He was given a blanket and a pillow, and he made his space on the cabin floor not far from the table at which he'd eaten. Even as he closed his eyes he doubted he would find sleep. Not with the images of Summer licking her lips and squeezing her breasts together from the back of the room.

But he did. He woke in the morning to find her outside at the well with a pout on her face.

"You don't like me no more, Balum?" She was raising the bucket by the crankshaft. Her breasts jiggled beneath her blouse with each turn of the handle.

"You know I do," he said. He came up beside her and took the wheel. He spun it. The bucket rose sloshing from the depths.

"You're just too sleepy for me," she teased.

He set the bucket over the well ledge. "I'm not too sleepy now."

She laughed. There were people in the streets. Several curious eyes flashed to the well. She looked right and left, shook her head. "You missed your chance, Balum," she said, and took the bucket and walked away. She gave her ass an extra wiggle. Before she turned the corner she glanced over her shoulder and blew a kiss at him and was gone.

When he rode out he saw no sign of Gary Cashews, but he did find a trail of hay scattered over the tracks that Kingston's carnival had left behind. He followed them past Margorie Dale's sagging homestead and he followed them where they swung wide of Canon City and the state penitentiary and all of its wretched memories blotting out the skyline there. He kept on them like a bloodhound on a coon trail. The same mentality. Like he'd gotten a taste of prey and wanted more. When he rode into Denver he even looked the part; unwashed and half-starved, his eyes bloodshot and his beard gone wild. The carnival was set up outside town but he didn't go near it. He let the roan clomp up the old familiar streets. Passerby threw him nervous glances. If it wasn't for the horse, he'd have been unrecognizable. A wild-looking man on a massive roan. Dragoon at his hip. Retribution in his eyes.

34

Ross Buckling lowered the paper he'd been reading and watched Balum cross the jailhouse and plop down in the chair across his desk. He showed no expression. Not until Balum took his hat off and set it over his knee. Then his eyes narrowed.

"Balum?"

"Shit, Ross. Maybe it's time you considered a pair of spectacles."

The sheriff tossed the paper on the desk and leaned forward. The chair squeaked beneath him. "Goddamn, don't you look a sight. You look like you've been through hell."

"If hell consists of Inglewood, Crenshaw, Fairview, and Muckville, and doesn't offer a lick of grub unless he sets to butchering hogs and chasing off squatters, then yes, I've been through hell."

"Ha! You just rode in?"

"Just now."

"And you came straight to see me?" Ross leaned back. Again the chair groaned. A sigh wheezed through his lips. "I'm guessing that means there's a heap of trouble riding in behind you. I reckon I know what it is, too."

"Is that right?"

"Joe came through here not more than a week ago. Had his senorita along with him. Pretty girl, that one. He filled me in. Told me all about this Big Tom fellow, his men trailing you. So my guess is there's three or four men hot on your heels, and they want you dead."

"Four."

"I knew it." Ross bobbed his head.

"Except they're already dead."

Ross's head went still. The chair went quiet.

"That trouble is all over with," said Balum. "I stopped in to see what you plan to do about the trouble that's already here."

"There's no trouble here."

"Didn't you get my telegram?" Balum raised a hand and swirled a finger around as if to lasso the entire city of Denver. "There's a pack of crooks in town right now, fleecing folks out of their money faster than a Tennessee tinker, and here you are reading the paper like it's Sunday afternoon."

Ross wrinkled his nose. "You mean the poker tournament?"

"No I don't mean the tournament. I'm talking about the carnival set up just outside town."

"Shoot, Balum, that's just good fun. Ain't no harm in that."

"You call getting your money stolen good fun?"

"Tell me when they ever stole anybody's money."

Balum explained. He went over the lost watch scam, the pyramid throw, the nail driving. He started in on the bucket toss and Ross shot a hand up and cut him off.

"Hell, Balum, I know half them games are crooked. Everybody knows it. But here's the deal. I can go in there and raise hell and run them off, but then what am I left with? I'll tell you what— a town full of angry citizens. See, given the choice between a crooked carnival and no carnival, folks will take the first."

Balum stretched his legs out. His hat wobbled over his knee. He let his elbows rest on the chair arms and shook his head. "What's Cafferty got to say about all this?"

"Pete? He's up in the North Country. Indian trouble." Ross was looking him over from behind the desk. "You could use some food, Balum. And a bath."

"I could use a plug of tobacco is what I could use."

Ross leaned down and opened a drawer and pulled out a pouch and tossed it over the desk. Balum took the first pinch, Ross the second. They sat in silence a minute, shooting tobacco juice at the spittoon in the corner.

"Are you going to let them go through with the crackshot deal?"

"The Kingston Crackshot? Course I am. It's set up for tomorrow night. I already bought my ticket."

Balum shook his head. He spat.

"Are you going to tell me that's crooked too?"

"It's crooked."

"How's that?"

"I've seen it done twice now, and I can tell you there ain't no way in hell that any sensible man would let Kingston go shooting at him. Not night after night. He's nothing but a damn tinhorn pretending to be a sharpshooter."

"So are you going to tell me how it's done?"

Balum leaned his head back.

"Well?"

"I don't quite have it figured yet." He came forward again. "Would you do anything to stop it if I did?"

Ross leaned forward and shot a stream of tobacco juice at the spittoon. He missed. He sat back in his chair, the wood squealing in protest. "Probably not."

"So you'll put up with underhanded carnival games," said Balum.

"For the good of the people."

"Fine. How about card cheats? Or have you let your sense of duty slip that far?"

"You know I don't put up with no card cheating, Balum."

"Good. Then let me tell you about a man named Rhett Hastings. He travels around with Kingston, him and a couple others. They're all wrapped up together in their chicanery. This Hastings is a first-class cardsharp. Maybe the best I've seen. And I can guarantee you he's in town right this minute, bottom dealing and culling the deck."

"Is he playing in the tournament?"

"I doubt it. His angle is to work on folks just outside of it. There's too many rules in the tournament, too many eyes watching."

"Do you have proof? You know how hard it is to catch a card cheat. Especially a good one."

"They rolled me over."

Ross tucked his chin to hide a smirk, but Balum caught it.

"What's that supposed to mean?"

The sheriff rose up and fired at the spittoon again. "Hell, Balum, we've all seen you play cards. A ten-year old girl could roll you."

"I'm serious, Ross. These guys are good. They work as a team. By the time they get through with this town they'll be a sight richer, and you're going to have some angry folks at your door asking why you didn't act."

"Shoot, I've already got angry folks at my door. Your friend Chester was in here a couple nights back grumbling about cardsharps."

"What did he say?"

"Oh, I don't know. Chester's a damn fine gambler. He's gone from living in a shack at the south end of town to wearing bow ties and top hats. The thing is, he's gotten used to winning. He has a bad night and he can't accept that maybe he got outfoxed."

"Was it Hastings? I sent him a telegram too. I warned him."

"He didn't say who it was. I don't think he even knows."

"Where is he?"

Ross waved a hand through the air. "Could be anywhere."

"I need to find him." Balum plucked his hat off his knee and stood up. He squared the hat over his head and spit the plug of tobacco out and gave a nod to the sheriff. He'd just reached the door when Ross called him back.

"I don't mean to pry, Balum, and you don't have to answer if you don't want to, but is there something wrong between you and Angelique?"

Balum turned around. "Something wrong?"

"I mean, it just strikes me as odd, that's all. You been gone how many months now, and the first people you look for is me and Chester. Seems you'd want to go straight to your woman."

"Believe me, I do. As soon as I see that Chester is alright, I plan on riding for Cheyenne, and I ain't gonna stop for so much as a sip of water until I get there."

Ross frowned. "You don't know?"

"Know what?"

"Angelique isn't in Cheyenne. She's here. She came in yesterday afternoon. She's got herself a room in the Rendezvous Hotel, right up there on High Street."

35

He might well have been mistaken for a runaway madman the way he leapt out of the sheriff's office and into the street, landing on his bloodstained boots with his spurs jangling and his hat clutched in one hand.

"I'll take the roan to Jackson Stables for you," Ross shouted after him.

Balum didn't answer. He charged down Main Street and into an alleyway and stumbled onto High Street where the fancier establishments rose like gilded towers over Denver. The pedestrians halted at his sudden appearance. A woman shrieked, a horse reared onto its hind legs. Balum halted. He looked right and left, the location of the Rendezvous Hotel momentarily lost on him. He chose left.

A covered porch girdled the hotel on three sides. Even from two blocks away he recognized it; it was the same hotel Suzanne Darrow and Leigha Atkisson had resided in, the same porch beside which he had vomited after a heavy night of drinking with Chester and Daniel. Memories fresh in his head. Memories of times gone by. Other days and other women, and none of them that could hold a candle to what he saw stepping onto the hotel porch with a parasol resting over her shoulder and a handbag held at her waist.

She might have noticed him for the fact that he was charging down the center of the street like a bull gone mad in a pole corral. Everyone else certainly did. They gave him a wide berth, pulled their children back. But the way she brought her eyes up directly onto him, so suddenly, it was as if some other sense was present; a connection beyond that of sight or sound that honed the two souls onto one another amid all the chaos of the city.

She dropped both bag and parasol. Spread her arms.

He crashed into her, the bull into his heifer, feral and savage and flagrantly obscene.

Mothers covered their children's eyes, men pretended to look away. The city of Denver held within its limits fourteen brothels and over fifty saloons— a city accustomed to debauchery, well-acquainted with public displays of affection— and yet the way Balum held Angelique beneath the porch awning, the way they kissed, how their hands ran over each other's bodies, it was unlike anything the townsfolk had ever seen. He was a soiled dirty beast fresh off the trail, and she a lady. When she took him by the hand and the two disappeared through the hotel door, the townsfolk stared after them like dumbstruck simpletons bewildered by an unreal and otherworldly event.

She did not undress him to rush him to the tub, though the suite came furnished with full washroom fixtures, and Balum sorely needed bathing. She undressed him to ravish him. To ride this wild beast that had journeyed over a thousand miles from the Texan grasslands to the Denver foothills, and all for her.

They made love on the bed and they made love on the hardwood floor. They made love braced against the wall and they made love again after he had finally scrubbed his body clean with lye soap and shaved the growth of two month's beard from his face.

They wore themselves down to nothing, and when they finally lay on the bed exhausted and blissfully naked, they held each other in their arms and recounted the lost days and all that had happened within them. He shared every detail of Buford Bell's escort south. Of Sara Sanderson. The hangings. She'd heard most of it only a week ago when Joe had arrived in Cheyenne, but she listened to it all over again. She laughed at his story of Lexie DeVries, grimaced at the tale of the dancehall ladies. In turn she told Balum of how a girl named Sadie had kept her warm at nights. She had met her at the Cherry Tree. A young girl with heavy dimples and an eager mouth. The details were enough to harden Balum's cock to the tenor of forged iron, and he rolled onto Angelique and sank his shaft into her for the fifth time that night as hungry as he had the first.

It was not until they woke in the morning that their conversation turned to quotidian things. Like what Angelique was doing in Denver.

"Don't tell me you came for the carnival," said Balum.

"I thought I might at least take a look."

Balum put a hand over his eyes. He groaned.

"Oh stop it," she pulled his hand away. "I didn't just come for the carnival. I came on business."

"Loans?"

"Yes," she traced her finger down his jawline.

He was looking around the suite. It was the finest room in the Rendezvous. "How far in advance did you have to reserve this room? The whole city must be sold out with the carnival and the poker tournament happening together. That's the way it was in Cumberland."

"I didn't reserve it. I arrived two days ago and asked for a room and they gave it to me."

He rolled his head sideways on the pillow. "Business must be good."

"It is. I don't know who had this room reserved before I came, but that's what happens when you're one of the biggest money lenders in all of the Wyoming Territory."

"That big?"

"Bigger than the Central Bank of Cheyenne," she said smiling.

"So who's getting the big loan?"

"Your friend Chester."

Balum sat up. The sheets fell across his hips. "What does Chester need money for? He's gotten filthy rich gambling. Last time I saw him he was duded up and buying rounds at the Baltimore Club."

"He's investing in a gambling hall. The opportunity came out of the blue, but with a time constriction. He wired me in Cheyenne and stressed how urgent it was. I don't normally lend on such short notice, and especially without a full review of a business plan, but he's such a good friend of yours, I decided to go ahead with it."

"How much did you lend him?"

"Four-thousand."

Balum's mouth gaped open but nothing came out.

"I know," said Angelique. "It's a big loan. But like you say, his reputation as a gambler has gotten around. An establishment of his own could net an enormous return."

Balum was already off the bed and pulling on his britches.

"Where are you going?"

"Get dressed," he said.

"What's the hurry?"

"You're right he's a friend of mine, and a damn good one. But he's a gambling man at heart, and there's no taking it out of him."

"You think he's going to gamble it away?"

Balum shoved his shirttails into his pants. "Right now there's a pack of cardsharps in town better than any Chester has ever run up against. He got rolled a couple of days ago—Ross Buckling mentioned it."

"He couldn't have lost four-thousand dollars in a poker game."

"Not in a square game. But this game is as foul as a bottle of Shane Carly's whiskey."

They checked the Silver Nest first. The main floor, then upstairs. They checked the Sagebrush. The Baltimore Club. Everything quiet. The hour was too early for the souls of gambling men, and what few faces stared back at them from those near-vacant establishments were blank and without answer.

They were halfway through a search of the restaurants and still no sign of him when they spotted Ross Buckling attacking a plate of steak and eggs through the window of the Berlamont Hotel. The steak was tough and the knife dull, and he'd come halfway out of his seat to better leverage the blade against the grizzle when he saw Balum and Angelique skirting through the tables. He lowered himself back into his chair. Let the knife clatter onto the plate.

"Either my knife is dull or my arm's gone lame. That, or they're down to serving breeding bulls past their prime." He shook his head at Balum and motioned to the knife. "You care to have a go at it? If you can cut that thing it's all yours."

"We'll eat once we find Chester," said Balum. "We've been all over and can't find him. Any idea where he is?"

The sheriff looked from Balum to Angelique. "I know exactly where he is. He's sitting in a jail cell about two minutes up the street."

"Huh?"

"That's right. The old codger lost his head last night. He'd have burned the town down if I hadn't put him away."

"What happened?"

"Another bad showing at cards is all I could make of it. He was drunk. Mad as a badger with his foot in a trap. Something about card cheats again. He don't normally carry a gun, but he'd gotten ahold of an old Mississippi Rifle and he was shooting it off every which way and cursing up a storm. I ain't keen on locking up old timers, but like I say, he'd have burned the town to the ground if I hadn't done something."

"Can we see him?"

The sheriff eyed his steak again. A slab of cold grizzled meat. "Might as well," he said. "I ain't gonna wrestle this piece of leather all morning."

They found Chester awake and brooding in his cell. He wore a collared shirt and a storebought sack coat, silver cufflinks, shoes lathered in black polish. The shirt was wrinkled, the polish worn thin, and he'd not shaved in several days. When he saw Balum and Angelique trailing Ross Buckling through the cell block, he covered his face in his hands and turned away.

Balum took hold of a cell bar. He leaned his forehead against the cold iron. He waited.

After a moment Chester peeked through his fingers. His eye went to Angelique. He closed it immediately and let out a soft whimper.

"Is it that bad, old buddy?" said Balum.

No answer.

"The money's gone, ain't it."

A little nod.

"We're gonna hear it sooner or later, Chester. So come on. Let's have it."

"I'm so ashamed," he mumbled into his palms.

"You want some coffee?"

Chester set his hands on his knees. He looked up. "I'd kindly appreciate that."

"Ross, open this cell up. Angelique, would you mind getting us some coffee?" He turned back to Chester, forlorn on his cot. "Come on, buddy. Let's get you out of there."

36

They sat all four of them around Ross Buckling's desk. Four chairs, four cups of coffee. One long story. Chester's story.

It started three nights ago in a musty gambling room on Gable Street where the saloons and brothels and gambling halls blended seamlessly one into another. The seedy side of town. The side Chester liked. He had anteed in with the idea of playing a few simple hands, a way to warm up his gambling mind in preparation for the tournament. The game was stud poker, four players, no limit.

Initially there was nothing wrong with the game, nothing that Chester could point a finger at. His cards weren't all that bad. Several hands were quite good. But the untalkative kid seated across from him seemed to always have better cards.

Over the course of an hour he lost over twenty dollars, more than he'd intended to gamble with in the first place, but his curiosity was piqued, and he kept on. He kept watching the kid. Watching his hands, his sleeves, his shuffles, his deals. He was fifty dollars in the hole when he caught the first mistake— a false riffle shuffle. Only it wasn't the kid, it was the fellow beside him.

"What did he look like?" Balum interrupted.

"Like a professional. Hair all slicked down, fancy coat. He had a way of rolling his chips over his knuckles, which irritated me. Maybe it was just supposed to distract me, I don't know. It worked though."

"That would be Frank. The kid works at the carnival. I'm guessing the third man was Rhett Hastings."

Chester sipped his coffee. His head shook slightly. "You're getting ahead of yourself."

"It wasn't Hastings?"

"Nope. The third man was short and dirty and drunk. Or pretending to be drunk. He wore an overcoat two sizes too big for him. I'd lay a dollar he was holding stacked decks in them pockets. His deals kept favoring the kid, just like Frank's."

"Barney Harrington."

"Yessir, I found that out later. But back to that night."

Chester took another sip. He continued. He knew he was sitting with cheats, so he cut his bets and instead focused on their sleight-of-hand. It was good stuff. False cuts and double dealing. A top card peek good enough to fool a country hillbilly. The whole thing riled him up so much that he would have liked to have shot them, but he wore no gun and he was no hand with one anyway. So instead he stormed off to see Ross Buckling.

He paused his story to scowl across the desk at the sheriff.

"Shoot, Chester," Ross flipped his hands up. "Maybe if you had explained it to me like you did just— calm and collected— I'd have done something."

"Well didn't I?'

"You came in here ranting like a madman."

Chester waved him off. The story went on. After complaining to Ross, he had wandered back to Gable Street with only a few vague ideas in mind, mostly absurd, all of them about revenge. But the three cheats were gone. So he took a seat in a quiet bar and ordered a mug of beer. In back of the room were a few poker tables, but the men playing were known as small-time cheats in Denver, and Chester wasn't interested in gambling anymore.

He was on his second drink when Rhett Hasting showed up. He sat down beside Chester, ordered a beer, struck up a conversation. Chester didn't feel like talking, but Hastings did. He told Chester he was a magician. He ran a little traveling show. Soon he had a deck of cards out and was showing Chester his tricks.

It was at that point that Chester's ears pricked up. The man was more than a magician, he was a sorcerer. He could tell Chester exactly what he was going to do— a bottom deal, a center deal, undoing a cut— and then he would carry out the sleight-of-hand two feet from Chester's eyes, and still Chester couldn't detect it. Nothing. It was the best card work Chester had seen in all his life, and he'd seen a hell of a lot.

It was at that point the man lowered his voice and confessed. He wasn't really a magician. He was a cardsharp.

"Rhett Hastings," said Balum.

"That's right."

"I warned you about him. Didn't you get the telegram?"

"I got it, I got it. You warned me not to play against him.

Well, I didn't."

Hastings never suggested playing against Chester. In fact, the opposite happened. He asked to play *with* him.

The reason Hastings gave for why he was sitting in a bar drinking beer with Chester instead of cheating folks from their money, was because his hot-headed partner had drunk too many glasses of *the liveryman's mare* over at the Sagebrush, which resulted in a broken nose, two broken tables, and a stint in the city jail. Now he was out a partner, and out of luck. He asked Chester if he was a gambling man.

Chester responded that he was, but he wasn't a cheat.

Hastings countered. He accepted that he was a cheat, but more a Robinhood-like sort of cheat. It wasn't in him to steal money from an honest man, he claimed, but to steal money from a fellow crook, why, he didn't see any harm in it. In fact, he thought it gave him a sort of respectability. A mission in life.

The con was simple. He and his partner would take seats at a game. They would play a while, let their fellow crooks get comfortable winning, and when the time was right Hastings would give his partner the signal. It would be on Hastings' deal. Every gambler at the table would end up with a fine-looking hand, but none that could beat his partner's. One big pot. It worked every time.

Chester was already hooked, he just didn't know it. Hastings ordered another round and asked him if he'd like to see it in action. He suggested the gamblers at the back of the room. Even from the bar Hastings could see they were stacking the deck. Poor card work.

Still, Chester wavered. Hastings persisted. He would put up his own money. Sixty dollars. He put his hand in his pocket and came out with a bankroll. He gave it all to Chester.

A minute later they were seated in the back of the room playing five-card draw with some of the most miserable cardsharps Chester had ever seen. It all worked just like Hastings had explained. They lost some hands, lost some money. The cardsharps got comfortable. When they got too comfortable, Hastings gave the signal; a stretch of his neck, and the deal was in play. Even though Chester knew what was happening, Hastings' work was too good to spot. Chester wound up with a straight flush. He bet hard, and the fools jumped.

A half-hour later the two were sitting in the Baltimore Club, surrounded by half-naked women, drinking fine whiskey, and splitting their winnings right down the middle. Just like Hastings had promised.

Drinks flow easy after a big win. Whiskey goes down smooth, it sits sweeter on the palate. Chester drank one, then another, then several more. He couldn't remember how their conversation turned to the three cardsharps that had rolled him earlier that night, but it turned out that Rhett Hastings knew them. He'd been cheated as well. It had happened a week ago in Muckville, and he'd ridden to Denver with revenge on his mind.

Chester perked up. As he remembered it, he sobered up right there. The truth was that he was drunk as a badger in a wine barrel, and not a single incongruency in Hastings' story gave him pause. The plan was to ditch the poker tournament altogether and lure the three cardsharps into a private game of high-stakes poker in one of the backrooms of Gable Street. They would work it just like they had an hour ago. Let them win some, then take it all in one big hand. The only problem was the money. Hastings' partner had it all.

Chester forgot about the naked women kissing his ears. He had money. He'd managed to save over a thousand dollars from his winnings. He would gladly bet it all.

But Rhett didn't like it. It wasn't enough. To convince the three sharps to abandon the tournament and play in a single backroom game, they would need a lot more.

And Chester could get it.

He stopped his story and threw Angelique a sheepish look. His coffee mug was empty. He set it on the desk and folded his hands. Head down, he told the rest.

There wasn't much to tell. Angelique arrived with the money. The game was scheduled. When it came time to play, Chester's nerves got ahold of him, and Rhett was right there with a glass of whiskey to calm them. It was not Chester's custom to drink while gambling— he was smarter than that— but this wasn't gambling. And so he drank.

He ended up sitting at a table across from Frank, Barney Harrington, the kid, and Rhett Hastings. Drinks all around. Women to distract him. And four-thousand dollars of borrowed money.

An hour later it was gone.

Looking back on it, it was easy to see all the steps where he'd gone wrong. But in the moment it had all seemed right. They lost a few hands, not big ones, just a little. Then the signal came. A stretch of Rhett Hastings' neck. Chester held a full house, and he bet like it was a royal flush. He went all in. Everything he had.

Frank took it with four aces.

Confusion followed. Confusion on the part of Chester, anger from Rhett Hastings. He pulled Chester into the street, shouting and waving his arms around. He claimed he hadn't given the signal, that Chester had ruined it all, that he never should have let a silly old man into his operation. He stormed off.

Standing there on Gable Street, drunk and broke and all alone, Chester put it together. He connected the dots. He went from drunk and confused, to drunk and angry. He stumbled home and fished out his old Mississippi Rifle, and the rest of the story needed no telling.

37

"I'm sorry, Angelique," Chester said into his lap. "I don't know how I'll ever pay you back. It took me years to save up those thousand dollars. To win four-thousand, why," he shook his head.

Angelique's voice, when she answered, came smooth and steady. No anger or reprimand, only the shrewd calculating tone of a woman with a mind for business.

"Do you still have your seat in the tournament?" she said.

"My slot was for last night," said Chester. "I gave it up. Besides, my bankroll is gone. I can't even buy in."

"What would you put your odds of winning at?"

Chester thought on it. Finally he shrugged. "I know what you're thinking. You figure maybe if you bankroll me I can win that tournament and pay you back. Only I can't. My head ain't in it no more. I can't take any more of your money and expect to gamble worth a damn. I'd only lose it all. Besides, the tournament winner only goes home with two-thousand." He shook his head again. His shoulders looked small, his frame shrunken.

Angelique looked at Ross.

The sheriff sputtered. "Hell," he shifted in his old wooden

chair. "That's gambling for you. There ain't nothing I can do about it."

"You can't arrest them?"

"Not without proof. I got Chester's story, and I believe every word of it, mind you, but as far as the law is concerned, you need more than that. More than a story."

"There is more," said Angelique.

"Is there?"

"All those men are part of the carnival. They all work together. Maybe you can't prove that their poker games are crooked, but the carnival games you can. Balum knows them all, don't you, Balum?"

Balum was staring at a spot on the floor. An old tobacco stain. He looked up.

"Like the pyramid throw," Angelique said. "Or the nail drive." She laid her hand on Balum's leg. "You know them all, don't you?"

"I know them," he said. He leaned forward. "You got any more of that good tobacco, Ross?"

The sheriff pulled the pouch from the drawer and tossed it over. Balum pinched out a wad and stuck it in his cheek. He leaned back and waited for the rush to sweep over him. It did. With it came a stream of thoughts. Clear thoughts. He turned to the spittoon sitting several feet away and spat. The gob hit the iron rim and sang out like a bullet ricocheting off a flat rock. Only there was no bullet. Just the sound of one.

"Balum?" Angelique said beside him.

Balum grinned. He looked around the desk at Chester, Ross, and Angelique, then he turned to the spittoon and aimed his fingers like a gun and fired. Another twang.

"You gonna tell us, or are you gonna spit tobacco all day?" said Chester.

"I can tell you all about their crooked games, but it won't do you any good," said Balum.

"It would get them arrested, wouldn't it?" Chester pleaded with the sheriff. "If you could prove them to be cheats?"

Ross's chair squeaked again. He was squirming.

"Ross don't want to ruin the fun for all the folks that traveled in from far and wide," said Balum. "He reckons they'd rather have a crooked carnival than no carnival at all. But like I say, it won't do any good. It may feel good, but that won't get our money back. And that's what we want, isn't it? Our money back?"

Chester agreed. Angelique agreed. Ross conceded that it was.

"The only way to get that money back is to win it back," said Balum.

"I can't," said Chester. "Like I say, my head's not in it."

"I don't mean poker," said Balum. "I mean at their own games. One game in particular." He launched another shot at the spittoon and grinned at the sound of the impact. "The Kingston Crackshot."

The three stared back at him. Blank looks all around.

"I've had time to think on it," he said. "Time to mull it over. It never sat right with me, the way Kingston handled that gun, or the way Frank always seemed so calm strapped to that wheel. Struck me as odd how much hay they needed to stop the bullets."

"Maybe they're just thinking of safety," said Ross. "A few extra bales can't hurt."

"Those bales aren't there to stop bullets."

"No?"

"There aren't any bullets to stop." Balum grinned. He couldn't help himself. He could see their minds working it over, trying to tie the pieces together just as he had, and coming up short. "That gun makes a loud bang, but nothing comes out. He's using cartridges loaded with powder, wad, and plug, but no bullet. No projectile. That's why Frank is so calm up there; he knows he won't get shot."

"But what about the holes?" said Ross. "Don't he leave bullet holes in the canvas?"

"Those holes are pre-cut. He likes to do his show at night, by torchlight. He keeps the crowd back a ways. Just far enough to see the holes when they appear, but not to study the canvas with any detail. The holes are cut out and held back up with wax I imagine, probably with a bit of string hanging from them. When Kingston fires, they appear. And that's where the hay comes in."

"What's the hay got anything to do with it?" said Ross.

"The hay is crucial. They stack it up like a three-walled fortress behind the wheel, tall enough to hide a man. Barney Harrington is my guess of who sits back there. All he has to do is grab a piece of string and pluck it off when he hears the shot. And there you go. There's your hole."

Ross whistled through his teeth.

Chester rubbed his eyes. He shifted around in his chair. "Well how are we supposed to use that against them?"

"We lay a bet that I can outshoot them," said Balum. "Like I say, those holes are pre-cut. They sit about eight inches from Frank's body. All I have to do is hit closer."

"Hold on," said Ross. "How are you supposed to get your holes cut in the canvas? And how will you get one of us hidden behind the hay? And do you even have any blank cartridges? I wouldn't even know where to find such a thing."

"I'll be using real bullets," said Balum. "I'll put real holes in the canvas. I'll outshoot him fair and square."

"Kingston will never allow it," said Angelique. "Not to mention Frank."

"It won't be Frank." Balum swung his head around to Chester. "It'll be you."

Chester stopped rubbing his eyes. He swallowed once. Swallowed again. "You mean tied up on the wheel?"

"If you trust my shooting."

Chester didn't answer. His face turned a strange shade of white and he tugged his collar away from his neck.

"Balum," said Angelique, "there's no way Kingston would allow it. Why would he accept a bet like that?"

"I agree with Angelique," said Ross. "A good con needs to be set up, needs to be planned. Kingston ain't no fool. Why would he take that bet?"

"He won't take the bet," said Balum. "He'll be the one making it. All I have to do is accept."

"How do you figure?"

"It's already been set up," said Balum. "The whole con, start to finish, and I'm the one who did it. I just didn't know I was doing it. See," he fired a gob of chaw at the spittoon again and turned back. "I've already bet them. Several times, in fact, and I've lost every time." He told them of his first encounter with Barney Harrington and Samuel Kingston. "They took me twice in the same night. Then they took me again in Cumberland." He walked them through his humiliation at the carnival games. "They see me as a sucker. An easy mark. Once he fires his five shots, I'll speak up loud and clear. I'll taunt him. One thing I learned in that carnival is that they don't like to be called out. They get defensive real quick."

"Still, Balum, why would he take a chance that you might actually outshoot him?"

"Because that part of the con has been laid as well."

He told them how he lost his Dragoon, how he ended up with the Colt Army revolver. He described his uneasiness with it. How that uneasiness had grown day by day until his confidence was gone and his own mind was set against him. He told them of his shootout with Andy Fletcher. How he missed. How lucky he'd been.

"The key part here is that Kingston's men saw me. Both Rhett Hastings and Barney Harrington were present. In their minds, I'm such a bad shot I can't hit a man standing smack in front of me. I'm just a simple fool who walks face-first into bets I'll never win. So once I start jawing, once I call him out and say I can beat him, he'll take it. He doesn't know anything about the Colt, and he sure as hell doesn't know about this," he palmed the Dragoon from his holster and laid it over the desk.

"What's that there?" Ross was pointing at the cylinder.

"That's from a Colt .45. A gunsmith down in Cumberland fashioned it up for me."

"So it takes cartridges," Ross nodded approvingly. "I'll be damned."

Angelique wasn't looking at the gun. Her eyes were on Chester who was breathing heavy and sweating down his collar.

"Chester," she said. "I know you feel guilty about what you've done, and you want to make things right. But you don't have to do this. It's not worth risking your life over."

Chester's lips had gone dry. He licked them. Tried to swallow. "It's just…" he tried to swallow again. "Aw, hell, I'm guilty. It ain't right what I done. I lied to you and I done lost your money, and I'll be damned if I let that go unaccounted for the rest of my life. Besides, I ain't scared. I know I look it, but I've seen Balum shoot. I seen him kill Lance Cain down in Bette's Creek, and I seen it when he shot Johnny Freed right out there in the street," he waved an arm at the door. "Balum, you're the best goddamn shot there ever was, and anybody who knows you knows that. What is it the Mexican's say about you?"

"*Donde pone el ojo, pone la bala.* Where I put my eye I put my bullet."

"And they're right." Chester emphasized this with a nod and a snort through his nose. "So I'll get up on that wheel. I'll let you put those bullets around me. Them men are nothing but greedy sons of bitches, and it'll do them right to sit on the short end of a con. How much money are you gonna wager?"

Balum rolled the chaw to the other side of his cheek. "Five-thousand. That's what we need, ain't it? Your own original bet, along with Angelique's four-thousand. You got that much, Angelique?"

"I've got it."

"Hot damn!" Chester tugged at his collar again.

"There's a problem though," said Balum. "That money's up in Cheyenne, ain't it?"

"In the Central Bank," said Angelique.

"That's about a hundred miles away, and the Kingston Crackshot happens tonight. There ain't no way a man can ride to Cheyenne and back before then."

"I'd put it up," said Ross, "but you know I ain't got that kind of money."

"Joe could bring it," said Angelique. "If we got a telegram to him quickly."

Balum shook his head. "By the time the telegraph operator gets it and sends someone out to the CW Ranch, finds Joe, and rides all the way back into Cheyenne, it'll be too late."

"But Joe isn't at the ranch."

"No?"

"He's staying at the Rosemont Hotel. He got it on account of Valeria— he didn't want to impose on Charles."

"Well shit," said Balum. He grabbed the Dragoon off the desk and slung it back in its holster. "We got a telegram to send."

38

They sent two; the first to the Central Bank, the second to Joe.

Then they waited. They stood outside the telegraph office and watched the wagons creak by. They watched a family of carnival goers argue over a limp balloon. They listened to Ross ramble on about the Indian problems in the North Country and how Pete Cafferty had his hands full, but no one really paid any attention. They were all waiting for one thing.

At the first sound of clicking from inside the office, Ross dropped his stories and they rushed inside. The message was from Joe. Three words only.

ON MY WAY

They marched back outside and stood a moment looking at nothing, looking at each other, looking at their four slim shadows stretched long by the morning sun. Hours to go and time to kill.

Chester suggested they get a drink.

"You want me full of whiskey when I start shooting?" said Balum.

"One for me then. To calm my nerves."

"It's too early. Why don't you go on back to the jailhouse

with Ross and try out his good tobacco. That'll calm you down some."

When they were gone, Angelique took Balum by the hand. "What about you?"

"You mean my nerves?" Balum shrugged. "Whiskey won't do it."

"I know what will."

It was an excuse that took them back to the Rendezvous Hotel. Good enough to while away a full hour in naked bliss. When they were both spent and lying naked on the sheets with their legs tangled together and their skin glistening in a sheen of sweat, Angelique took his chin in her hand and turned his head to face her.

"Tell me what's wrong."

Balum took hold of her breast. He squeezed it. Licked her nipple. "I'm a sex-crazed demon and I can't get enough of you."

"Stop it," she laughed. She slapped his hand. "I'm serious. What's wrong? Are you worried about Chester?"

"I can put those bullets right up against Chester's head; I'm not worried about that." He rolled onto his back and looked at the ceiling. "It's Kingston. I can sucker him into a bet, I can outshoot him, I can get our money back. But I want more."

"You want to ruin him."

He rolled toward her. Her eyes were dark. They saw into him, through him. It was the same way she'd looked at him when they'd first met.

"Ross thinks the townsfolk would rather have a crooked

carnival than no carnival at all, but I don't buy it. I think they'll put up with a game that's a little uneven, but not out-and-out fraud. I want to show them who he is."

"What do you think they'll do?"

"If Ross is right, they won't do much. Grumble a bit. Forgive him."

"And if you're right?"

Balum set his hand on her hip. He smiled. "If I'm right, there's gonna be hell to pay."

By sundown over a thousand people were gathered in the carnival grounds. The first to arrive secured the best spots; right up against the ropes at the foot of Kingston's platform.

Balum did not count among them. He was pacing back and forth on the northern edge of town where the road to Cheyenne disappeared into the foothills. An empty road in the falling evening.

"It's going to start soon." Angelique pulled him around. "We need to find Chester and get in place."

Balum's eyes wandered back up the road.

She took his hand. "You know him well enough. He'll be riding bareback with a string of fresh horses alongside, and he won't slow down when he switches mounts. He'll be here."

The jailhouse door was closed and locked when they reached it. A quick search of the Silver Nest and the Sagebrush turned up nothing. They looked in Jackson Stables and checked the Rendezvous, the bars on Gable Street and the tables at the Baltimore Club. In the end they found him slumped over a glass of mezcal in the old Mexican cantina. The barman with the heavy mustache recognized Balum. He pointed Chester out.

"He say he pay later, but I no care. *No importa. A un amigo de Balum no le cobro.*"

"He'll pay you, alright," said Balum. He heaved Chester up by the arm. "He's just got to earn it first."

They walked on either side of him, holding him by his arms to keep him steady. Once out of the Mexican barrio and past the barbershop on Dade Street, he got his feet under him.

"I can walk," he drawled. "I was just calming the old nerves, is all. I'm alright."

"Where's Ross at?"

Chester looked around confused. "Where's Joe?" he answered.

They didn't ask again.

By the time they reached the carnival grounds, Kingston had already given his speech, and his assistants were tying Frank to the wheel. Over a hundred torches had been lit. As Balum and Chester and Angelique pushed through the crowd, Balum studied the orange glowing faces. There existed some seed of doubt yet. If Barney Harrington was among them, his theory would fall apart. And that's all it was, really; a theory.

But he didn't find him. He didn't find Joe either. He spotted the rat-faced lawyer William Claddy. He recognized Judge Vanderloop. He picked out the receptionist from the Rendezvous. He saw Shane Carly sharing a bottle of drink with another man, and Balum nearly tripped when he recognized who it was. The red pony-tail gave it away.

"Balum, hurry," Angelique pulled him forward.

A gunshot cracked across the night. A gasp followed. When the wheel slowed enough for the crowd to see the small dark hole eight inches from Frank's elbow, they let out a wild yell as if collectively drunk on Shane Carly's rotgut. Kingston bowed. The wheel spun again. He fired twice, two sharp cracks, and two more holes appeared.

Balum kept looking, kept searching. His eyes were hunting a face darker than the rest, a throat marked by a long wicked scar, long black hair and tar-black eyes. He'd half-forgotten about Ross when he spotted the sheriff waving his hat from the edge of the crowd.

"Where is he?" Balum shouted over slouch hats and bonnets.

Ross only raised his hands.

"Find him!"

Another shot. The fourth.

Chester stumbled. Balum reached back and caught him by the shirtfront and pulled him through the rabble, working himself through the crowd like a wedge inching through hardwood, Balum the point, Chester and Angelique on his flanks. He was almost to the platform when Kingston fired his last shot. The crowd went silent. All eyes on the wheel. It slowed to a stop, and there between Frank's knees, the fifth hole.

Samuel Kingston twirled the revolver around his finger and slunk it back in its holster. The move made Balum cringe. Only a goddamn fool played with a gun that way. He shoved a step closer and ignored the looks thrown his way.

"A hand for my assistant!" Kingston gestured to Frank, who took a few dizzy steps, then stopped and bowed. "A brave man. But how could he not be, when it is I, Samuel Kingston, the single greatest crackshot in living history, on the end of the gun!"

The populace roared. Kingston made a few more bows while he waited for quiet to return. When it did, he opened his mouth to speak, but Balum cut him off. His voice was deep, a voice often described as gruff, and when he wanted to he could project it like a war cannon. He did just that.

"You're no crackshot." His voice sailed over the crowd. "You're a cheapshot. A tinhorn. There's half a dozen men right here who could shoot better than that."

Kingston stopped his prancing. He squinted at his audience. "What do we have here? Ah, yes. A cowpoke full of bluster, eager to impress his lady."

"Just a man telling the truth," said Balum. "Someone who actually knows how to handle a gun would have put those bullets closer. Not you though. You're lucky you didn't kill that man."

Kingston stopped scanning the crowd. His eyes found Balum. The recognition was obvious.

"Like I say, half a dozen men here could shoot better," said Balum.

"Like who? Like yourself?"

Balum didn't answer. Instead he looked away. He gave a half-hearted shrug. He'd been swindled enough to know how it was done. The way a good con worked was not to force it on the mark, but to lead the mark into it. And so he played dumb.

"Probably," he mumbled.

"Ha!" Kingston laughed. "Look how the bluster leaves him! All talk, and nothing to back it up with."

"I'll back it up," Balum raised his voice again. "Put your man back on the wheel."

Kingston grinned at the crowd. "Our cowpoke here must think I'm a fool. And Frank as well. Frank," he swiveled around, "would you let this sodbuster go shooting at you?"

"No sir!"

"Of course not. A man would have to be drunk or a fool to agree to that."

"My friend here will," Balum grabbed Chester by the arm and raised it up. Chester lurched forward, off balance.

Kingston's lips turned down. His head cocked sideways. Then he laughed. "Of course! Just as I said; a drunk!" He stopped laughing and shook his head. "You'd only kill that poor friend of yours. I'll not turn my wheel into an execution by firing squad."

"That's because you know I'd beat you."

Kingston shook his head. His temper was rising. Being called out was a bad note to end on, and he wanted a way to finish it. To put Balum in his place.

Balum gave it to him.

"I'll bet you five dollars I could shoot better."

The amount was comically low. If Kingston had stopped to think about, he might have seen it for what it was; a trap. Bait. But he didn't. He snapped at it.

· "Five dollars!" he shouted to the crowd. "Five dollars is what the cowpoke comes back with. Whoa, big spender!" The crowd laughed. A few woops went up. Kingston hooked his thumbs in his belt and leaned back. "If you were to put up real money, I'd take that bet. But you don't have any. You're broke and busted, and all you've got is a big mouth. Even if you did have it you wouldn't risk it. You know you'd lose. You've just seen a man whose skill is superior to your own, and all you can do is brag and blather and create a scene."

"Five-thousand dollars." Balum's voice cut into the night.

The throng had been laughing and casting insults, and when he shouted the full figure of his bet, they fell silent.

Kingston's scowl returned. He unhooked his thumbs from his belt. "You don't have it."

"He's got it right here!"

Kingston turned. The crowd turned. At the edge of the torchlight Joe sat bareback over a jet-black stallion, sixteen hands tall and covered in a rich lather of sweat. His hand was raised, and in his hand a leather satchel. He gave the stallion a nudge and walked it forward through the crowd, clear to the stage. He tossed the bag. It landed at Kingston's feet.

"You said yourself you'd take that bet," said Balum. "Like I said, I'll put my own man up there. Your own assistants can tie him up and spin the wheel. Or does the great crackshot want to admit he's nothing but a fraud?"

From the middle of the crowd someone shouted: "Take the bet! He ain't no hand with a weapon. He can't hit a barn door when he's standing in front of it."

Balum craned his neck around. He couldn't see the face,

but he recognized the voice. Gary Cashews. Just like Ruth and Eva had said, he liked to start rumors.

"I seen him myself," Gary went on. "I seen him handle a gun. He was all doped up on laudanum, just like he is now."

Before Kingston could answer, Rhett Hastings ducked through the ropes. He climbed onto the platform and whispered something in Kingston's ear. Barney Harrington followed. He appeared out of nowhere, suddenly in the torchlight, hay still clinging to his clothing. He joined the two on the platform. Whispers and plotting. What they were saying, Balum already knew.

"Fine," said Kingston. "Tie him up."

"Show the money first," said Balum.

Another blow to Kingston's gut. His face reddened further, but he gave the order. In the time that it took for his men to ready the money, the crowd made their own bets. Gary Cashews invented more lies. Chester was led wobbling to the wheel, his arms and legs spread, and his face a pale gray.

Balum ducked through the ropes and climbed the platform and met Chester's eye. One hard look, and then the wheel was spinning. They put their strength into it, and Chester's arms and legs turned into a blur. Like a clockface speeding through time.

Balum drew. The old familiar feel of the Dragoon handle. The weight, the balance. The hammer in the right place.

He fired.

A woman in the crowd screamed. Her shriek ended and there was nothing left but the sound of the wheel and the crackle of torch fires. It slowed. The crowd surged forward.

Before it came to a stop, a torrent of green bile sailed from Chester's mouth. It cut an arc in the air and splattered in the dirt at the base of the wheel.

The response was a groan from the onlookers, quickly turning to a cheer as they realized that Chester was alive, and building louder when they saw the fresh hole beside Chester's elbow. It wasn't more than two inches away.

"Spin it again!" shouted Kingston. "Two shots this time before it stops. Just like I did!"

They spun it again. Fast. Balum fired. He put the first bullet beside Chester's other arm, pulled the hammer back, and put the next one between his legs.

When the wheel stopped, Chester's face had gone from gray to white. His eyes rolled in their sockets, his lips quivered. If there was anything left in his belly he would have spilled it. The wheel only stopped long enough to verify that the shots had beaten Kingston's, and then Chester was spinning again, a strange wail curdling from his throat. Only the head shots remained.

Balum didn't wait for Kingston's goading. He didn't think about anything really. He let his body take over. Reflexes, motions long memorized, repeated a thousand times over.

Two shots. They boomed in the torchlight, faded out into the Denver foothills.

Chester went quiet.

There might have been two-thousand people gathered in attendance, and not one of them made a peep. One giant breath was held. The wheel stopped. The two fresh holes had come so close to Chester's ears, they'd almost drawn blood.

The crowd let their breath out in shouts and hollers and wild cowboy yells. Chester came off the wheel. He staggered to the right and bent at the waist and puked again.

Balum raised both arms to the crowd. He meant to quiet them, but they only howled louder.

"Quiet, now," he shouted. "Quiet! Listen here," he pointed at Kingston standing red-faced beside the platform. "What do you say we give him another chance? An easy way to win back all his money."

A multitude of confused faces peered back from the darkness.

"You got one shot left in that gun, Kingston. You say you're a crackshot. I say you're a fraud. So I'll tell you what. I'm going to give you all your money back. All you have to do is hit that wheel." He pointed at it. An eight-foot wide drum of empty canvas, no more than thirty feet away.

"Go on, Kingston. I don't care where you hit it, just so long as you put a hole in it. Anywhere. And I'll give you all five-thousand back."

Kingston's face had lost its red tint. A sheen of sweat covered it. Cold sweat. His eyes went from Balum to the two mounds of money sitting on the platform, and over to the empty wheel. He swallowed.

"Now why won't he take that bet?" Balum asked. He looked over the puzzled faces. "Don't he want his money back?"

No one had an answer. Not even Gary Cashews.

Balum jumped off the platform. He landed beside Kingston. One quick movement was all it took to strip the

Colt .45 from Kingston's holster. He ran back up the platform and held it up to the crowd.

"I'll show you why!" he shouted, and turned the gun on Kingston and fired.

The boom of the gun coincided with another shriek in the crowd. A woman fell. Arms raced to catch her. Eyes went everywhere; to the woman, to Balum, to Kingston. When the woman regained her feet, Samuel Kingston was still standing, the gun barrel still smoking.

"No bullets," Balum explained. "A big bang, nothing more." He came off the platform again and crossed the thirty feet to the wheel. He grabbed the top one-handed and heaved down, splintering the wooden brace that held it upright. What was left in its place was a little cave filled with boot prints. He pointed to Barney Harrington. "Why do you think that man over there is covered in straw?"

"You mean he wasn't even shooting?" someone hollered.

"He's a fraud," someone shouted back.

"It's all a fraud," said Balum. "Why do you think none of you could drive a nail into a log with one strike?"

Silence.

"Because he filed the points off the nails."

"I lost four dollars in that game," came a voice.

"I lost six," said another.

A woman pushed forward. "They're nothing but a pack of thieves!"

"I want my money back," someone yelled.

Kingston was already backing away. Frank and Barney and Rhett Hastings backpedaled out of the torchlight. Some of

Kingston's assistants started for the wagons, and someone in the crowd shouted: "Don't let them get away!"

As if on signal the crowd broke. They stormed through the ropes and ripped torches from the ground. Kingston ran for the wagons. Barney and the rest followed. They didn't make it halfway before the mob cut them off. They veered for the hills instead, running on foot, nothing but the clothes on their backs and whatever they had in their pockets. The mountain of hay went up in flames behind them, the wagons and the tents and the booths, the entire carnival blown into a whipping conflagration, and by its light the swindlers fled into the night, chased by a mob two-thousand strong and riled to the point of madness.

Balum did not join them. Nor did Angelique or Ross or Joe. Chester hadn't fully recovered his balance. He sat in the dirt holding his head.

"You alright, buddy?" Balum set a hand on his friend's shoulder.

"I'm alright."

"That's a hell of a thing you did, getting up on that wheel. You got a gambling man's nerves, I'll give you that."

Chester rubbed his belly. "I got an empty belly is what I got."

"Let's go fill it then." He pulled Chester to his feet.

Joe had stuffed Kingston's money into the leather satchel. He handed it to Balum. "Aren't those the same jokers we ran into in Inglewood?"

"They're the same."

Joe smiled. "You've got a story to tell then, don't you."

"I got more than one. How about I tell it to you over a steak? All of you. You've earned it. Even you Ross."

The sheriff stood with his hands on his hips. He was staring at the flames shooting skyward. He turned around. "Who's going to clean all this up?"

"Shoot," said Balum. "Maybe if you give me a plug of that good tobacco of yours, I'll even help." He put an arm around Angelique. "We'll worry about it in the morning. Right now we've got some living to do."

They turned toward town. The shadows cast by the fire danced across the dust before them. Four dancing shadows. Smiles on every one.